Daniel's eyes were fierce with emotion

"You left me, but now you'll come back knowing I own you."

"You can't own human beings," Lindsay stammered.

His eyes flashed with bitter humor. "Can't you? If you want to save your brother's neck, you'll come back to me. And on my terms."

"You're crazy. You won't get much enjoyment out of forcing me to—"

"Won't I?" he asked. The next second he had one arm around her while the other forced up her chin.

"Don't," she whispered, and Daniel's eyes glittered as he smiled in threat.

"That's one word you'll never use with me again." His mouth came down on her lips, burning with a fever she felt leaping up inside herself. The demand of the kiss was met by an answering demand in her. She was out of control....

CHARLOTTE LAMB

the sex war

Harlequin Books

TORONTO • NEW YORK • LONDON
AMSTERDAM • PARIS • SYDNEY • HAMBURG
STOCKHOLM • ATHENS • TOKYO • MILAN

Harlequin Presents first edition October 1983
ISBN 0-373-10635-1

Original hardcover edition published in 1983
by Mills & Boon Limited

CHAPTER ONE

LINDSAY was in the shower when the phone rang, and she was half inclined to ignore the ringing, but it might be Aston to say he couldn't make their date, so with a sigh she stepped out of the shower cubicle, pulled on her short white towelling robe and ran down the corridor to the sitting-room, leaving wet footprints on the carpet everywhere she trod. Snatching up the phone, she said breathlessly: 'Hallo?'

'Lindsay, it's Alice.'

'Oh, hallo,' said Lindsay, feeling water trickling down her spine from the wet tail of red hair clinging to her nape. 'I was in the shower and I'm very wet, Alice, is it urgent?'

'I'm sorry, I didn't . . . I just wanted . . .' Her sister-in-law sounded incoherent, which was unusual for Alice; a placid, quiet girl whose only interests seemed to be her home and family. Alice's brown eyes and hair both had a red-russet tinge which, coupled with her demure manner, always reminded Lindsay of a squirrel watching everything from a safe distance but with bright-eyed interest.

'Is anything wrong?' Lindsay asked, clutching the lapels of her robe.

Alice seemed to hesitate, then she asked unsteadily: 'Is . . . is Stephen with you?'

'Stephen? No, he isn't here. Is he coming to

see me?' Lindsay turned her head to look at the clock on the mantelpiece. Aston would be here in half an hour. They were going to the theatre and she didn't want to be held up.

Without answering her question, Alice asked another of her own, her voice even more shaky. 'Have you seen him since yesterday?'

'No.' Frowning, Lindsay wondered what this was all about, but before she could ask Alice audibly sighed.

'He hasn't rung you, you haven't heard from him?'

'No, I haven't.' The urgent note in Alice's voice seemed very disturbing, Lindsay gripped the phone tighter. 'Is something wrong, Alice?'

'If he's talked to you, tell me, Lindsay, don't lie to me, please!'

'Why on earth should I lie to you? I haven't heard from Stephen for a week or so, he rang me in the middle of last week and asked when I was coming over. I said I'd try to come and see you all soon.' Lindsay had never interfered in her brother's life, nor would she have allowed him to interfere in her own, but she was very fond of Stephen and something in Alice's voice worried her. 'Have you and Stephen had a row?' she ended uncertainly.

'He's disappeared,' said Alice on what sounded like a sob.

'Disappeared?' Lindsay felt a dart of shock. 'What do you mean, he's disappeared? Since when?'

'He didn't come home from work last night, and he hasn't been at the factory at all today, nobody seems to know where he is.' Alice stopped, swallowing audibly. 'Lindsay, I'm so worried, I don't know what to do, I'm going out of my mind!'

Lindsay stared absently at the wallpaper a few feet away from her, her eye following the curve of a green branch from which tiny pale pink rosebuds broke. She didn't quite know what to ask, how to respond. Alice's news had come as too much of a shock. Stephen had seemed quite normal when he talked to her last week. He hadn't said anything which might alert her to any change in his usual behaviour. Stephen was the last person she would have expected to disappear without warning; he was an even-tempered, cheerful man whose life seemed very much under control.

'Have you rung the police?' she asked at last, falling back on the purely practical.

'No, not yet. I wasn't sure if . . . should I? He's only been gone for twenty-four hours, there could be a perfectly rational explanation, he might have left a message that didn't get passed on. If he turns up he'll be so embarrassed, he'll be furious with me for getting into such a state, and I'll feel a fool if I've made a fuss over nothing.'

'Is he in his car?'

'Well, yes, he went off in it yesterday morning, anyway.' Alice drew a sharp breath. 'Do you think he might have had an accident?'

'Could be,' said Lindsay. Failing any other explanation that would have been the first thing that came into her head. 'Did he have anything on him to identify him? If he did have an accident, that is . . .'

'I don't know, I suppose so, he usually has his credit cards and driver's licence in his wallet.' Alice sounded as though she just wasn't thinking clearly, which was hardly surprising in the circumstances. 'And it's hours now since he left the factory yesterday. It isn't like Stephen, he always comes straight home.'

'He could have gone off on urgent business and forgotten to let you know,' Lindsay pointed out gently.

'It isn't like him.' Alice sounded as though she was on the point of tears and Lindsay had a strong suspicion that there was a great deal which her sister-in-law wasn't saying, but as she couldn't see her face she could only guess at that.

'I was in the shower, it will take me ten minutes to get dressed,' she said firmly. 'I'll be with you inside an hour, then we'll decide what to do.'

'Oh, thank you, Lindsay.' Alice's voice trembled, was husky. Lindsay had said the right thing, Alice's call had not been so much a check on whether Stephen had been in touch with her as a wordless cry for help. Alice couldn't cope with whatever was wrong between her and Stephen, and that didn't surprise Lindsay. She had always guessed that all the strength in that marriage came from Stephen, her brother had always been someone you could rely on, and Alice had leaned heavily on him from the start. Whenever you saw them together, Alice kept close to him, listened while he talked, had very little to say for herself, left all the decisions to him. If Alice was a secretive little squirrel, Stephen was a broad oak in which she sheltered.

Lindsay rang off and went back into the bathroom. She dried her hair roughly, got dressed in a formal white silk blouse and tight-waisted, pleated black skirt, then blow-dried her hair into the style she liked best, the red-gold strands gleaming loosely around her face, in a casual light wave. She had just finished doing her make-up when the door bell rang. She knew it was Aston, he always gave three short rings. He was early, which was just as well, she wouldn't have to leave a note pinned to the front door for him.

'Hallo, gorgeous,' he said as she opened the door, and held out an enormous bunch of flowers; roses, carnations, freesias, their scent masked by the polythene envelope holding them.

'They're beautiful—thank you,' said Lindsay, smiling, as she accepted the flowers. 'Come in, I'll put them in water before they wither.' She walked back into the kitchen and Aston followed her, closing the front door behind him. Her flat was on the second floor of a large block of service flats in central London. The rooms were tiny, just big enough to swing a cat, but they were modern and comfortable and she was within easy walking distance of the West End.

She filled a large, green-glazed pottery jar with water and unwrapped the flowers, while Aston leaned against the wall watching her. Over her shoulder, Lindsay said apologetically: 'I'm sorry, Aston, I'm going to have to break our date tonight. Something's come up—family troubles.

I've got to go over to see my sister-in-law, she just rang me and asked me to come at once. I'd have tried to get in touch with you, but . . .'

'What's wrong?' Aston asked, frowning. He wasn't exactly a good-looking man; but his rugged face had strength and humour and a very distinct personality. His hair was a goldy brown, the colour of a new penny, coppery bronze, and his eyes were hazel and smiled a great deal. For a very big man, over six foot and built on muscular lines, he walked lightly and moved with grace, but there had been nothing subtle about his interest in her. He had begun to pursue her from the minute they met, bombarding her with phone calls and dropping in at her flat without warning all the time. Lindsay had begun by giving him the cold shoulder; she had been in no mood to encourage any man when she met Aston and when her icily polite refusals did not have any effect she had been forced to tell him bluntly that she wasn't interested, so goodbye. It hadn't made any difference that she had noticed. Aston had kept on turning up, amusement in his face, as though Lindsay's snappy rejections merely made him laugh. His water-dropping-on-a-stone technique was irresistible. Lindsay started to laugh, too, in the end, and found herself saying: yes, instead of: no way!

'My brother seems to have done a bunk.' Lindsay was briskly pushing the flowers into the vase, her eyes on their colour, her nostrils assailed by their muted scent. 'There, how do they look?' she asked, turning back to Aston.

'Nice,' he said. 'What do you mean, he's done a bunk? Left his wife?'

'I'm not sure what he's done, Alice wasn't very coherent on the phone. I'm sorry about the theatre tickets, Aston, maybe you could find someone to go with you? A pity to waste them.'

'That doesn't matter,' he said, shrugging the suggestion aside. He was a man who talked with his body, his broad shoulders and hands in movement when he spoke, like an Italian. 'Where does your brother live? I'll drive you over there.'

'That's very kind—are you sure?'

'Get your jacket and we'll be on our way,' he said, grinning at her. Lindsay smiled back wryly; it was typical of Aston to take charge of whatever was happening. He was an organiser to his fingertips, he ran his life the way he ran his firm; with humour and determination and unstoppable energy which did not make him disliked by his employees. He had several shops in London, selling electrical goods. Lindsay had met him through her brother, who manufactured electrical components. Stephen had made friends with Aston at an international trade fair in Germany two years ago. They did not deal directly with each other on a business level, they were merely drinking companions on occasion.

His car was parked outside the flats, a sleek Ferrari with an engine that purred like a cat and could eat up the miles without really trying. Aston liked fast cars and good clothes and, not being married, could afford them. He slid Lindsay into the passenger seat, closed the door on her and walked round to get behind the wheel.

As he drove off with a roar, he asked quietly:

'Stephen in some sort of trouble? Or is it a private matter?'

'I told you, I have no idea at the moment what's wrong. I suspect he and Alice have had a row, but she wasn't saying on the phone. I can't think of any other reason why he should go walk-about.' She looked sharply at Aston, her dark brows lifting. 'Unless you know different? Have you heard something? His factory isn't in trouble, is it?'

'We're all in deep waters these days.' Aston wasn't looking at her and his face was not giving anything away, he watched the road as though afraid to take his eyes off it. 'There's a recession, in case you hadn't heard.'

'Stephen's been hit by the recession? He hasn't said anything. At least, not to me he hasn't.'

'Would he?' Aston put the question very gently and she sighed.

'I suppose not, he does tend to hug his problems to himself. Stephen never forgets that he's my big brother.'

'He's about five years older than you, isn't he?' Aston asked, tongue in cheek.

'Seven, do you mind?' She laughed and Aston turned his head to smile at her, eyes teasing.

'Which makes you . . .?'

'Twenty-five.' Her glance mocked him. 'I've packed a lot into my life, if you're wondering how I got so wise at my age.'

'I wasn't actually. I was thinking that Stephen looked much older than thirty-two. I'd got him down as nearer forty.' He put on speed, frowning again. 'His face is quite lined. How long has he been running the factory?'

'Since my father died. Stephen was nineteen, then, and the factory only employed three or four men. Stephen began to expand about five years ago. Now he employs around forty.' Lindsay was very proud of her brother's business achievements. She had only been twelve when her father died, and within three years her mother had been dead, too; of pneumonia caught because she neglected a bad cold. Mrs Grainger had stopped caring about her health after her husband's early death. His heart attack had been a bitter shock to her from which she never recovered. Left alone to carry the family, Stephen had taken over at home as well as in the business. Stephen hadn't married until after Lindsay left home, and brother and sister had been very close. Their relationship might appear outwardly offhand and casual, but although they were neither of them openly affectionate they cared very much what happened to each other.

'Five years?' Aston repeated. 'I suppose that was around the time . . .'

'I got married,' she agreed flatly.

'Did Randall take an interest in your brother's firm?' Aston sounded very casual, but she felt him watching her out of the corner of his eye.

'Financially, you mean? I don't think so. It has always been a family firm, Stephen wouldn't have wanted to part with any shares, even to Daniel.' Lindsay laughed shortly, her face derisive. 'Not that Daniel Randall would have been interested in a firm as small as Graingers—quite out of his league, they have to be pretty big fish for him to start angling for them.'

'I'd have thought that as Stephen is your brother——' Aston began, and she cut him short, shaking her head.

'I can tell you don't know Daniel. He'd be the first to tell you that sentiment has no place in business.' She paused. 'And how!' she added with emphasis.

'I've heard that he's ruthless.'

'Who told you that? It must have been a friend of his—it's far too generous. Daniel Randall is red in tooth and claw. He doesn't merge with other firms, he devours them and spits out the pieces, and he doesn't care who gets hurt in the process. I'm grateful for the fact that Graingers didn't arouse his attention, it was just as well for Stephen. Heaven knows what would have happened after I divorced Daniel Randall if he had had any hold over the firm.'

'You don't like your ex-husband much, do you?' Aston asked wryly, half smiling as he drew into the kerb outside the modern white house where Stephen and Alice lived.

'Like him? Boy, is that an understatement!' muttered Lindsay, swinging her long legs out of the car. 'I loathe the man!' She walked round to join Aston, the light from a street lamp gleaming on her red-gold hair, and he looked down at her with appreciation, his hazel eyes very bright.

'I'm glad I don't have to worry about competition from that quarter, any way,' he admitted. 'When you kept turning me down, I did wonder if you still hankered for him. He's a good-looking guy, it wouldn't have been surprising if you had still carried a torch.'

'For Daniel Randall? Do me a favour, I have too much sense. I was too young to know what I was doing when I married him, but once I'd found out how devious he really was I lost no time in making my escape.'

Aston laughed. 'How green your eyes look at night, like an angry cat's. I wouldn't like to feel your claws!'

'As long as you realise I've got them,' said Lindsay, sliding him a wicked look from beneath her lashes.

'Oh, I'd noticed them. You made sure I did right from the start, didn't you? I was paying Randall's bill, was I?'

'I was off men then,' she agreed, shrugging, as she started to walk up the drive to the front door of the house.

'And now?' Aston asked, catching up with her after a second's pause. 'How do you feel about men now?'

Before she could answer, the front door flew open and Alice stood in the doorway with the light behind her, staring at them eagerly for a moment before the light in her eyes went out and her mouth trembled in disappointment.

'Oh, it's you, Lindsay.' It was obvious that she had thought it was Stephen returning, no doubt she had heard the car and jumped to conclusions. She was pale, her usual colour absent from her small face and her hair was ruffled and untidy. It looked as though she had flung on her clothes without thinking; her jeans were creased and shabby, her red shirt had come out of the waistband of the jeans and the top button of it was missing, her neckline giving a clear vision of her small breasts. She looked amazingly young, almost childish, and Lindsay could see she had been crying; her brown eyes were red-rimmed, her eyelids puffy.

'No word from Stephen yet?' Lindsay asked, giving her a quick kiss on the cheek, and noting the cold dampness of her skin.

Alice shook her head, then looked at Aston. 'Have you seen him?' Again that eagerness, that nervous pleading in her voice.

Aston said gently: 'No, but don't worry too much, there could be a hundred explanations of why he hasn't been in touch with you.'

Alice went back into the house and Lindsay and Aston followed her into the sitting-room. It was very untidy; toys were scattered on the floor, children's books open on the couch, a large red setter dog padded to meet them, his tongue lolling out, and barked in token threat before allowing Aston to rub his head behind those long, silky ears.

Alice watched him, her expression uncertain. She did not know Aston very well and was always very quiet in the company of someone unfamiliar to her. Shy and wary, she was more or less the same age as Lindsay but gave the impression of being much younger, perhaps because she had married Stephen only a year after leaving school and had seen very little of the world outside her home. Her first baby, Matthew, had been born only eighteen months after she and Stephen got married, and little Vicky had followed her brother just a year later. Alice hated leaving her children in the care of babysitters, even Lindsay was barely acceptable to her as a mother-substitute, it was on very rare occasions that Alice allowed Lindsay to take over from her. Most nights, Alice and Stephen stayed at home together, listening to music, watching TV or reading. Alice was very far from being an outgoing girl, and Lindsay could see that Aston's arrival had disconcerted her.

'Why don't we make some coffee?' Lindsay suggested, and her sister-in-law looked at her gratefully. 'Like some, Aston?' Lindsay asked, and Aston looked round, smiling, still playing with the dog.

'I'd love a cup of coffee.'

'We won't be a minute, clear a space on the couch and sit down.'

Alice looked embarrassed. 'I'm afraid the place is very untidy, I haven't had time to . . .'

'Doesn't matter, it looks cosy and lived-in,' said Aston, giving her a comforting smile. As Alice hurried out of the room, Lindsay gave him a wry grimace.

'I'm not famous for my tact, I should have realised she'd be touchy about the way the room looks, but with small kids around nobody can keep a house tidy for long.'

'Go and talk to her,' Aston said. 'She looks as though she's in the middle of a bad trauma.'

'Yes,' Lindsay agreed, sighing. 'I wonder what on earth has been happening?'

'Marriage,' said Aston drily, and she made another face.

'Oh, yes—why do we do it?'

She found Alice in the kitchen laying out cups with a dull expression, her movements slow. Lindsay watched her with compassion and uneasiness. What had gone wrong between her and Stephen?

'What was he like yesterday morning?' she asked, and Alice jumped, looking over her shoulder with open distress.

'What? Oh, Stephen, you mean?'

'Who else? Weren't you thinking about him?'

'I was wishing I knew what to do—I feel so helpless, not knowing where he is or what's happening to him. How can he do this to me?' The cry broke out of her suddenly, her voice rising, and her body trembled, she caught hold of the back of a chair and leaned on it, her head hanging down.

Lindsay put an arm round her and felt the tremor running through her. 'Now, calm down and try to think. Have you two quarrelled? Come on, Alice, you can tell me, these things do happen in the best marriages, you know. Was there a row?'

'No,' Alice said vehemently, lifting her head so that Lindsay could see her face. 'What would we quarrel about? We never quarrel, Stephen isn't the quarrelsome sort, neither am I.'

That was true enough, Lindsay thought, watching her. She never remembered hearing the two of them come anywhere near having a row.

'Is Stephen worried about the firm?'

Alice hesitated, biting her lip. 'I don't know, he never talks about work, he never has . . .'

Lindsay caught the faint hint of something

unspoken in her voice and frowned. 'But?' she
pressed.

'But what?' Alice broke away from her and
went over to make the coffee as the kettle boiled.
Her hands were shaking, the spoon rattled against
the sides of the cups as she spooned instant
coffee. Lindsay looked at the ruffled red-brown
hair, the curls tangled and lifeless as they
clustered on Alice's thin nape, and she felt an
impatient sympathy for her sister-in-law. Alice
was waiting for someone else to tell her what to
do, as Stephen had always told her what to do
until now. Any self-confidence Alice had ever felt
had apparently atrophied during her marriage—
what you never use you may well lose entirely.
Lindsay understood how Alice felt, she might
well have gone the same way if she hadn't
divorced Daniel Randall, she thought. Daniel had
wanted to rule her life the way Stephen had
always run Alice's life for her, but Stephen's
motives had been generous and tender. Lindsay
wouldn't say the same for Daniel.

'Come on, I picked up something from you just
now—do you suspect that Stephen's worried
about the firm?'

'I'm not sure.' Alice put the cups on to a
formica tray. 'I don't know, he didn't talk about
it, but there was something wrong with him
lately. He was always sitting about staring into
space, always in a daydream—he had something
on his mind, but he wouldn't talk about it.' A
little flush had crept up into her face, it burned
along her high cheekbones. Lindsay stared at her,
frowning.

'Didn't you have any idea what was wrong?'

Alice's voice was harsh when she spoke. 'I thought there might be someone else.'

Lindsay's eyes opened wide. 'Another woman?'

Alice turned on her suddenly, speaking quickly and angrily. 'Well, it happens, doesn't it? And look at me.' She flicked a dismissive hand down herself, her mouth bitter. 'I'm always a mess, I haven't got much energy. Matt and Vicky beat me into the ground most days, by the time Stephen gets home I'm worn out, I hardly have enough life to do more than say hello and put his dinner in front of him. I flop out on the couch all evening and crawl upstairs to bed like a zombie. I can tell you, there isn't much fire in what goes on in our bed these days. If Stephen has fallen for someone else I wouldn't be amazed.' She stopped talking and bit her lower lip to steady it, then said: 'But he might have rung me before going off with her.'

'Who . . .' Lindsay began, and got a brief look. Alice's eyes were far too bright, there were unshed tears behind them.

'No idea. His secretary is a married woman of fifty with a daughter older than me—it certainly isn't her. I talked to her several times today, and she's as worried as I am, she wanted to ring the police this morning.'

'I think she's right,' Lindsay said. 'That's what we ought to do.'

'Stephen would never forgive me if . . .'

'Stephen isn't here to forgive you or otherwise, and we're wasting time. The sooner we tell the police the better, they can check up and find out if anyone of his description has been involved in an accident. Stephen could be lying in some hospital ward, unconscious—anything could have happened to him. He could have been mugged and all his belongings stolen, or . . .'

'Don't!' Alice protested shrilly.

Lindsay sighed. 'It's the only sensible thing to do, Alice. You must see that.'

After a long silence, Alice nodded slowly.

'Would you like me to ring the police?' Lindsay asked, and Alice nodded again. 'Right, then you take Aston his coffee while I get on the phone, and don't look so worried, it may turn out to be . . .' She stopped speaking as Alice walked out, carrying the tray, the cups clattering together.

The police were polite but made no pretence of being seriously concerned. 'We'll check the hospitals, miss,' the duty sergeant at the local station said. 'But unless he's been involved in an accident there isn't much we can do. He could be anywhere. It happens all the time, you know, men walk out on their families without saying a word and just disappear into thin air. But we'll do our best. Give me a few details about him. How tall is he?'

'Five foot nine or ten, I think.'

'Colour of hair?'

'Dark red.'

'That's unusual, might be a help,' the sergeant said. 'Long or short, is it?'

'Short, Stephen keeps it very neat and well-trimmed.'

'Colour of eyes?'

'Hazel—more green than brown.'

'And distinctive marks? Moles? Birthmarks?'

'He has a mole on his neck just under his ear.' Lindsay felt sick suddenly, she had a feeling she was describing a man she would never see again. Until that moment she hadn't been taking Stephen's disappearance seriously, but now her stomach plunged with anxiety.

'What was he wearing?' the sergeant asked.

'I don't know, I'll have to ask his wife.' Lindsay put down the phone and went into the sitting-room. Alice was sitting on the edge of a chair, her hands clasped tightly in her lap. Aston was trying to make conversation, but Lindsay got the feeling it was uphill work.

Alice had to think for a minute before she could answer. 'His dark grey suit, a blue-striped shirt and a blue tie,' she said, and Lindsay went back to repeat that to the policeman.

'What sort of car was he driving?' she was asked. 'Could I have the number?'

Lindsay could answer that without checking with Alice, Stephen had often driven her home to her flat after visiting them. Her voice wasn't quite steady as she answered and the policeman said soothingly: 'Now, don't worry too much, miss, it's a hundred to one he's perfectly safe somewhere. Sometimes a man feels he has to get away to think things out.' He paused. 'Is there anyone at the factory we could contact? Anyone in his confidence who might have an idea why he's gone?'

'His secretary? I could ask my sister-in-law for her name and address.'

'Would you do that, miss? It would help.'

'Hang on,' said Lindsay, and went back to Alice, who frowned in a distracted way.

'I've spoken to her, I told you, she doesn't have any more idea than I do . . .'

'It won't hurt for the police to talk to her,' Lindsay said. 'What's her name?'

Alice shrugged wearily. 'Mrs Temple, she lives in the new close behind the factory—I don't know the number of the house; I remember her telling me how pleased she was when she moved in because the house was so compact. I thought she was crazy, it was a rabbit hutch.'

'Watford Close, miss? Right, we'll see if we can talk to Mrs Temple tonight. Will someone be with Mrs Grainger? We might call round to have a chat, it depends if I can spare a man. We're light-handed tonight.'

'I'll be here,' said Lindsay, and rang off a moment later, her spirits very low. Talking to the policeman had made Stephen's disappearance real. Where could he be and why had he gone?

She went slowly back to join Alice and Aston, who looked round at her in question. 'No news?' Aston asked. Alice said nothing, but her eyes were like holes poked in a white sheet, her lips were colourless and trembled. Lindsay sank down on to her knees beside her sister-in-law's chair and held her shaking hands tightly.

'It's going to be okay, don't look like that.'

'What will I do if he never comes back?'

'Of course he'll come back, you mustn't think like that!'

From upstairs came a thump and a wail. Alice

jumped to her feet. 'Matt's fallen out of bed again.' She was out of the room and running up the stairs a second later. Lindsay heard her voice in the small bedroom which the children shared; soothing, calming, in a murmur. Getting up, Lindsay joined Aston on the couch, her hands linked behind her head and her body relaxing with a sigh.

'I could kill Stephen! If he was worried, couldn't he have talked to us about it? Did he have to clear off like this? He must know what it's doing to Alice.' She turned her head and Aston touched her cheek with one hand gently.

'Don't get so upset, it's early days yet, he could walk in through the front door any minute.'

Tears welled up in Lindsay's eyes, she buried her face against Aston's shoulder. 'I'm scared,' she whispered. 'It isn't like him. Stephen's always been so strong. What if . . . if something has happened to him?' She couldn't bear to put her fears into words, but she was afraid that Stephen might not ever come back. She might have brushed aside Alice's worry, but secretly she was beginning to feel the same—how could you help being afraid when you didn't know what had happened? The fear of the unknown prompted all sorts of dark ideas, suspicions, dreads.

'Ssh . . . Alice is coming,' Aston murmured. 'Don't let her see you like this, you've got to put a brave face on it for her sake, Lindsay.'

Sitting up, Lindsay brushed a rough hand across her wet eyes and Aston slid his arm round her, squeezed her comfortingly. They heard Alice coming slowly down the stairs, then another sound caught their attention, a car engine which shut off as they sat up. Lindsay stiffened and began to get up.

'Stephen!'

'It could be the police,' warned Aston.

They heard Alice running. Lindsay went to the door just in time to hear Alice fumbling with the lock on the front door, then it was open and a cold wind blew into the little hallway. Lindsay stared in rigid disappointment at the stranger facing Alice, whose thin shoulders had slumped as she realised it was not her husband.

'Mrs Grainger? Has Mr Grainger come back yet?'

'No,' Alice said in a husky voice.

'How long has he been missing, Mrs Grainger? Can I come in and talk to you?' The man was young, thin and sallow-skinned, wearing an old sheepskin coat. He smiled at Alice and flicked a quick look at Lindsay over her shoulder as he began to insert himself into the house, talking fast. 'Have you any idea why he's disappeared? Is there any trouble at his factory or . . .'

'Who are you?' Lindsay cut across his sentence. 'Are you from the police?'

She saw his hesitation, then he smiled charmingly at her. 'I won't take up much of your time,' he began, and Lindsay interrupted again.

'Are you a reporter?'

'Oh!' Alice gasped, falling back from him.

'Isn't Mr Grainger related to Daniel Randall?' the young man asked, ignoring Lindsay's question and keeping his eyes on Alice, obviously deciding she was the softest target.

'Out!' snapped Lindsay, advancing on him and pushing him back through the front door. 'Go on, get out, we have nothing to say to you.' Mention of Daniel was a red rag to a bull, she was flushed and very angry.

'All I want to do is help you find your husband,' the reporter protested.

Lindsay shut the front door in his face. Turning to look quickly at her sister-in-law, she found Aston in the hall, watching her with a wry smile.

'You're a tough little lady, aren't you?' he mocked. 'I thought for a minute you were going to hit him.'

'So did I,' Lindsay muttered through her teeth. 'What a nerve, trying to talk his way in here!'

'You haven't got red hair for nothing, I suppose,' Aston commented.

Lindsay put her arm round Alice. 'Come and sit down. Have you eaten tonight? Are you hungry?'

'No,' Alice whispered. 'How did that man know Stephen was missing? Who could have told him?'

'He probably picked it up at the police station, reporters always have a contact in the police,' Aston said. 'And I'm hungry, Lindsay.' He gave her a plaintive little smile and she laughed.

'Okay, you talk to Alice, I'll get us a meal.'

'I'm not hungry,' said Alice.

'Nobody's going to force you to eat if you don't want to,' Lindsay said, giving Aston a secret look. He steered Alice back into the sitting-room and

Lindsay went into the kitchen to see what she could find.

She was no more hungry than Alice was, but she felt it would do them all good to have something to occupy their minds while they waited for news. No doubt Alice hadn't touched food all day, she looked hollow. While Lindsay scrambled eggs and grilled tomatoes, made toast and more coffee, she was trying to think of some place Stephen might head for if he was in trouble. As small children they had always had holidays in Cornwall, might he go there? She mentally made a list of their relatives, but their family had never been very close and Stephen had often told her how much he resented the total indifference of their aunt in Yorkshire, their uncle in Scotland, when their parents died. Nobody had come to help Stephen then, they had appeared at the funeral, drunk some sherry and made soothing noises then departed without making any offer to help. Stephen would be very unlikely to look for help from any of them now.

She carried a loaded tray into the sitting-room and practically force-fed Alice, who was still reluctant to eat but managed to get down some of the scrambled egg and a half slice of toast. While Aston and Lindsay drank the last of the coffee, Alice wandered over to the window and stood, the curtain drawn back, her nose pressed against the glass like a hopeful child, waiting.

Lindsay collected together the plates and cups. Aston took the tray from her and carried it out into the kitchen. 'Are you staying here tonight?' he asked, and she nodded.

'Of course. You'd better go now, Aston. I'm very grateful for your help, you've been very kind.'

'Sure you wouldn't like me to stay tonight?'

'We'll be okay. I'll to get her to go to bed soon, she looks worn out. I've got some sleeping pills in my handbag, I'll give her one of those.'

'Do you need to take sleeping pills?' Aston asked, frowning and eyeing her in surprise.

'Not often, but I had insomnia after my marriage broke up and now and then it comes back.' She flushed as she met his eyes. All that was behind her now, she preferred not to remember the anguish Daniel had put her through, the black nights when she lay awake and ached for him, the long-delayed dawns which brought no hope of any end to her pain. When you are trapped in bitter, hopeless feeling you always think there can be no escape from it, but Lindsay had freed herself at last. She had begun to sleep regularly, without dreaming of Daniel; she had woken up without that dead sense of depression.

Aston's face gave no hint of his reaction, he merely nodded. 'I see.' He looked at his watch. 'I'd better be on my way, then. If you need me, give me a ring, don't hesitate to ask. You know I'll do anything I can.'

She smiled at him and stood on tiptoe to kiss him. 'I know—thanks.'

He put his head round the door of the sitting-room to say goodnight to Alice, who looked at him in startled surprise. 'Oh, yes, goodnight, thank you for . . .' Her voice trailed off and Aston smiled at her.

'Try to get some sleep, remember your children will need you tomorrow.'

Tears came into her eyes again and Lindsay pushed Aston down the hall. 'Sorry, said the wrong thing,' he whispered, and she shook her head, then opened the front door.

'Of course not, don't be an idiot. She's just off balance.'

He caught her head between his hands, looked down into her face, his hazel eyes smiling. 'Did I tell you I think you're gorgeous and I'm crazy about you?'

'Goodnight, Aston,' Lindsay said.

He kissed her mouth lightly, then released her and walked out of the house into the dark night. She stood in the doorway, a yellow stream of light falling down the drive in his wake, and watched him climb into his car. The engine flared and he drove off. Lindsay closed the front door and went back to Alice who was sitting on the couch staring at nothing, her legs curled up under her, her hand propping up her head.

As Lindsay sat down next to her, Alice said; 'If I only knew what had happened to him, where he was . . . not knowing is the worst, I think I could even stand it if I knew for certain he had gone off with another woman or just left me because he was tired of me. I could bear anything but this, I keep trying to think, going round and round in circles getting nowhere.'

'You ought to try to get some sleep—you're exhausted. I'll stay up in case there's any news and I'll come and wake you if . . .'

'No,' Alice said. 'I couldn't sleep, I'd never be

able to close my eyes. I can't shut off my head. Lindsay, what if he's d . . .'

'Don't say it!' Lindsay said sharply, wincing. 'Don't even think it, of course he isn't.'

The door bell rang briskly. Alice stumbled to her feet, white as a sheet, her eyes widening until her skin stretched tightly over her cheekbones. She looked old, suddenly. Lindsay wanted to cry, but she forced herself to stay calm.

'I'll go, it's probably the police to ask you a few questions,' she said.

She took a deep breath before she opened the front door. What if the police had bad news for them? There was no point in thinking about it. She pulled the door open and made herself look at the man on the doorstep, only to feel a deep thrust of shock as she recognised him. Even in that shadowy light Daniel Randall was unmistakable, then he stepped forward into the yellow light from the hallway and his hard-boned, arrogant face came into full view. Lindsay was stricken, she couldn't speak or move, she half believed she was imagining things. He was the very last man she had expected to see.

CHAPTER TWO

'CAT got your tongue?' Daniel looked at her stunned face with a derisive smile, and the question broke the spell of disbelief holding her rigid. She felt a wave of hot colour rushing up to her hairline. What was he doing here? She hadn't set eyes on him for over a year, why had he turned up like this tonight?

'What do you want?' She stepped sideways to block his way; she didn't want him walking into the house and saw no reason why she should pretend he was welcome.

'As quick-witted as ever, I see,' he drawled, and the way he spoke was all too familiar. Daniel Randall always used that slow, iced voice when he wanted to make someone feel stupid; he was a past master at destroying people and using the simplest means to do it—a lifted eyebrow, a smile, a drily succinct comment.

Lindsay wanted to hit him, and that feeling was familiar, too; hostility was the safest emotion to feel towards Daniel Randall.

'What the hell do you *think* I'm doing here?' he asked before she could say anything. 'And are we going to stand here much longer? I'm not a door-to-door salesman, I don't enjoy talking on people's doorsteps.'

Over his shoulder Lindsay saw his car parked under a street-lamp, a sleek, powerful white sports car with elegant lines which had been carefully designed for effortless speed. For some reason, the sight of it annoyed her.

'Get back in your car and hit the road, I've got nothing to say to you,' she snapped, closing the door. Daniel's foot met it and the door jarred. Lindsay glared at him through the opening. 'Go away!'

'Don't be a fool, Lindsay,' he said, and at that moment a car roared up behind his and parked with a screech. Someone leapt out of it and Daniel looked round, frowning.

'Get inside,' he said to Lindsay, thrusting her back into the hall with a violence which stopped her arguing. Daniel followed her and slammed the front door behind him.

'What . . .' Lindsay began furiously, and he gave her a sarcastic smile.

'Want to talk to the press, do you?'

Her mouth opened and nothing came out. The front door bell rang, but Daniel ignored it. He walked towards the sitting-room, catching Lindsay's arm en route and pulling her in his wake, struggling to free herself without success. The door bell went on ringing and Alice stared at them, pale-faced, wide-eyed, nervous apprehension in the way she stood there.

'What's wrong? What's happening? Aren't you going to answer the door? Lindsay . . .' Her voice died away as she recognised Daniel.

'Hallo, Alice,' he said in a gentle voice, and smiled at her. When he chose, Daniel could give out charm and warmth; his grey eyes held both now, and Lindsay resented the way Alice relaxed and smiled back.

'Daniel! I didn't realise it was you, how are you?'

'I'm fine, how are you? Any news of Stephen yet?'

Her lower lip trembled and she caught it between her teeth, her eyes too bright. 'No. . . .'

'How do you know Stephen's missing?' Lindsay asked suspiciously, staring at him.

He turned that wry glance on her, his eyebrows raised. 'A reporter told me.'

'I thought you never talked to reporters.'

'I wouldn't have talked to this one if he hadn't convinced Henshaw that I'd want to speak to him.'

'Really?' Lindsay asked with sarcasm in her voice. 'That was clever of him, how did he do that?' Daniel's London home was run by a married couple who were far too well trained to talk to the press. What could a reporter have said to one of them to make them think Daniel would want to speak to him?

'He told Henshaw you were in serious trouble and the police were involved,' Daniel said drily, and Lindsay was stunned.

'He did what?' She was so angry she could scarcely speak, and Daniel laughed briefly at her expression.

'Once he was actually put through to me, of course, he came across with the truth about Stephen vanishing; by then he'd achieved his object.'

'What a rotten trick!' Lindsay exclaimed and Daniel shrugged.

'You should know by now that reporters can be unscrupulous in pursuit of a good story.'

'You're a fine one to talk about scruples,' Lindsay muttered, turning her anger in his direction. 'You wouldn't know a scruple if one came up and bit you!'

'Watch yourself!' There was the hiss of rage in Daniel's soft voice, and Alice took a step backwards in alarm, but Lindsay refused to budge, meeting his cold stare without blinking. She wasn't afraid of him, she meant him to know it, and her chin lifted defiantly. Other people might back off when he gave them that narrow-eyed look; in the past she had often done so too, but not any more, he needn't imagine he could frighten her with that air of controlled menace which he was so expert at giving out.

How did he do it? It wasn't just his height and build, other men of his physical type didn't have that effect—it was the mind behind that tautly structured face that was so disturbing.

Just over six foot, Daniel Randall was lean and tightly muscled; a man with a deep chest and wide shoulders which breathed power, but whose height added elegance to the impression he left, those long slim legs and supple hips moving with grace. Lindsay had often watched people watching him, seen the way women's eyes followed him. At first it had made her glow with pride, but in the end she had resented it; it underlined for her the fact that Daniel Randall was not a domesticated man, he was not cut out to be anybody's husband, he was a ruthless predator at home in the jungle of his own choosing.

Alice had backed until she sat down on the couch. Daniel detached his eyes from Lindsay and went over to sit down next to Alice, taking one of her hands between both of his.

'Now, Alice,' he said, one long sinewy thumb stroking the back of her hand in a soothing rhythm, 'what's this all about? Why has Stephen gone off?'

'I don't know,' said Alice, her voice high. She was grey, tired, her eyes great pools in that colourless face. 'He didn't come home last night, that's all I know.'

The door bell rang again, someone had his thumb on the bell and wasn't lifting it. Daniel turned his head, a flash of rage in his eyes.

'I'll knock that guy's teeth down his throat if he keeps that up much longer!'

'Maybe it's the police,' said Alice, stiffening.

'It's the reporter who was here before,' Lindsay told her in a flat tone. 'I recognised him.' She glanced at Daniel and then away. 'He must have been the one who rang you. He tried to talk his way in here earlier and I shut the door on him.'

Daniel detached himself from Alice, getting up. 'What are you going to do?' Lindsay asked, frowning. 'Don't lose your temper, if you hit him it will be all over Fleet Street tomorrow morning.'

'I'm going to ring the police,' Daniel said curtly. 'Alice has a right to be left alone in her own home, they can send someone over here to keep the press away.'

'They're shorthanded,' Lindsay told him.

'They told me so when I rang to tell them Stephen was missing. They won't be able to spare anybody to stand outside here all night.'

Daniel stared at her, then turned and went out. Lindsay followed and watched him pick up the phone. 'What are you going to do?' she asked again, and he gave her a dry smile.

'I'm getting a couple of men to mount guard over the house until this blows over.'

He dialled and Lindsay went back into the sitting-room, hearing his deep cool voice talking in the hall as she sat down next to Alice.

'Stephen won't like it if this gets into the newspapers,' Alice warned.

'He should have thought of that before he went off without telling you where he was going.' Lindsay found herself see-sawing between worry about her brother and impatience with him, her fear kept turning into anger and she could understand why Alice wouldn't go to bed. How could anyone rest when their husband was missing? She heard Daniel replace the phone and walk back towards them. Her reactions to his appearance on the scene were confused too; she was relieved to have him take charge and start organising events, but she was irritated that he should feel he had the right to do so. It was all part of that calm arrogance which she found insupportable—who did he think he was?

'I've got some sleeping tablets in my bag, why don't you take one and try to get some sleep, Alice?' she asked her sister-in-law, who frowned petulantly, her forehead lined.

'I couldn't—no, how can I go to sleep not knowing . . .'

Daniel halted in the middle of the room, listening. 'That's a very good idea,' he said, cutting into her stammered sentence. 'Give Alice the pill, Lindsay. Alice, go upstairs, have a warm bath and get into bed, then Lindsay will bring you some hot milk and you can take her pill and get off to sleep.'

Alice would have argued, but he bent and took her arm in a firm grip, hoisted her to her feet and smiled at her.

'If Stephen was here, that's what he would tell you to do. We'll wake you up the minute there's any news.' He led her to the door and Lindsay followed, watching them wryly. His cool assumption that Alice would obey him was maddening, especially as it was working. Alice reluctantly began to climb the stairs. She paused as the door bell rang again and Daniel said: 'Off you go, Alice,' his voice insistent. Alice went, dragging herself upwards like a weary child. Looking round, Daniel said to Lindsay: 'Get her that milk and stay until she's taken her pill, make sure she swallows it.'

'Yes, sir,' Lindsay muttered through her teeth, bristling, but her antagonism merely made his brows lift.

'Don't you want her to get a few hours' sleep?'

'Of course I do, I just object to being ordered around as if I was a halfwit.'

He smiled. 'Well, you said it. Anyone with any sense would have got her off to bed hours ago, she's on the verge of breaking up into a hundred little pieces.'

'Do you think I couldn't see that? I tried to talk her into going to bed, but she wouldn't hear of it, and I could hardly make her go.'

'I managed it,' shrugged Daniel, and Lindsay felt like screaming, his self-satisfaction put her teeth on edge. She turned on her heel and went into the kitchen to heat some milk. Daniel came into the room a moment later, he had shed his smoothly tailored camelhair overcoat and was running a hand over the ruffled black hair as she turned to look at him.

'Now that we've got Alice out of earshot, tell me what you know—why has your brother gone off like this?' He got a kitchen chair and sat down on it, astraddle, his arms folded across the back of it and his chin resting on the dark sleeves of his formal suit. She wondered what he had been doing this evening—had he been dining out? A business evening, or a private one? Had he been with a woman? The elegance of the suit, the crisp white shirt and wine silk tie suggested that he had been with a woman, but Lindsay refused to think about that, it was none of her business any more.

'I don't know any more than Alice. Stephen didn't come home from work last night and there hasn't been a word from him to explain why he's gone away. Alice says they haven't quarrelled, she doesn't know about any business worries he might have, she hasn't a clue why he's gone.' Lindsay watched the milk beginning to bubble in the small saucepan. 'She did say she wouldn't be surprised if it was another woman, but I don't believe it. Stephen isn't the unfaithful sort.'

'What sort is that?' Daniel asked drily. 'He's a

man, isn't he? He isn't a saint, it could happen to anyone.'

'Don't judge my brother by your standards!' snapped Lindsay with a bite in her voice. The milk was beginning to boil now, she took the saucepan off the hob and poured the milk into a tall glass, stirred it with the spoon. 'Stephen loves Alice, I don't believe this has anything to do with another woman. I think it's something to do with the business.'

Daniel nodded, his chin still on his arms. 'You're probably right. What was the name of that accountant who worked at the factory? The old guy with the grey hair and rimless spectacles?'

'Mr Datchet?' Lindsay was surprised by his memory. She hadn't even thought of asking Henry Datchet, although now she realised that if there was any trouble at the factory he would know all about it.

'Datchet,' agreed Daniel, nodding as he stood up. 'That's the guy. Take that milk to Alice, I'll get in touch with Datchet and see if he can provide any answers.'

She followed him into the hall, balancing the milk on a saucer. 'I don't know his address.'

He picked up the telephone directory, giving her a sarcastic smile. 'I'll find him,' he said, and Lindsay went upstairs without a word. She was sure he would—Daniel Randall always managed to do what he wanted to do.

She found Alice just climbing into bed in a short pink nylon nightie printed with little white flowers. She looked small and helpless and

childlike as she settled against the pillows, her
russet hair damp from her bath, the edges of it
curling around her pale face.

'Drink this and take the pill, then try to sleep,'
Lindsay said gently. It was hard to believe that
the girl in the bed was the mother of two
children, her usual quiet confidence had all been
erased by worry.

Alice took the pill reluctantly, sipped the milk,
her throat moving as she swallowed it, then she
lay down and Lindsay switched off the light.
'Goodnight, we'll be downstairs if you need us
and we'll wake you up the minute there's any
news.'

She heard Alice sigh as she closed the door,
then Alice turned over and the bed rustled.
Lindsay quietly went downstairs.

Daniel was still talking on the phone, propping
himself up against the wall with one brown hand.
His skin was slightly sallow and took the sun
easily, retained that tan longer than most people
seem to do, which threw his light grey eyes into
more prominence, their silvery gleam sliding
sideways to watch Lindsay as she walked past.
She felt a shiver run down her spine and looked
away. She did not want to be aware of Daniel
Randall in that way; there was too much sensual
assessment in his glance. She felt it even with her
back towards him, those cynical eyes seemed to
burn a hole into her head.

'I see,' he was saying. 'That would explain it,
of course. How much leeway does he have?'
There was a little silence, then he whistled softly.
'Mr Datchet, could you come over here first

thing tomorrow morning with the books? I think
we should have a quiet discussion with the
figures in front of us.'

Lindsay stood just inside the sitting-room,
listening, her brows drawn.

'I understand and I admire your integrity,'
Daniel said a moment later, 'but I assure you it
will be in Mr Grainger's best interests, Mrs
Grainger will be here, you could talk to her
before you talk to me.' He paused again, then
said: 'Yes, of course. I perfectly understand your
position, but this is a matter of urgency. Don't
you agree? If it will help you to make up your
mind, ring the bank, ask their advice—after all,
it's their money which is at stake.' Another
silence, then he said: 'Good, I'll expect you at ten
o'clock, then. Goodnight, Mr. Datchet.'

A moment later, Daniel sauntered into the
sitting-room, his hands in his pockets, whistling
softly, the lazy air of satisfaction he wore making
Lindsay's nerves jump. She didn't trust him,
particularly when he smiled to himself like that.
What was he up to?

'Well?' she demanded, and he eyed her with
distinct mockery.

'Well, what? Oh, Datchet? He was being pretty
cagey, but he did admit that Stephen had a hefty
bank loan outstanding which falls due in a week
or so. Datchet wraps everything up in sub-clauses
like a lawyer, but I gathered that Stephen didn't
have a hope in hell of repaying it and he's been
trying to raise the money for weeks without any
success. Until I see the books I won't have any
idea whether the firm's on the rocks or not, but

it's clear enough that Stephen is in serious trouble. Datchet seemed very worried.'

Lindsay sat down. She felt cold, she thought of her brother desperately struggling to raise the money to repay that loan and she wanted to cry. What do you ever know about other people? Stephen hadn't given her any idea that all this was on his mind, he had been wearing a bright smile whenever she was with him, yet all the time he must have been out of his mind with worry.

'Why didn't he say something?' she asked, mostly talking to herself. 'Why keep it to himself? Not even to tell Alice—how stupid can you get?'

Daniel shrugged, cynicism in his smile. 'Alice is the sort of woman men try to protect, she can't take pressure, as we see.'

'What would you know about Alice?' Lindsay flung back at him with barbed hostility. 'About any woman, come to that?'

His smile died away, and the grey eyes hardened. 'Don't snarl at me, Lindsay. I'm only trying to help your brother.'

'Accepting help from you is like taking it from a tiger,' Lindsay said bitterly. 'When you offer to help someone, you usually end by swallowing them whole. Stephen won't have a company at all by the time you've finished with him.'

'Thank you,' he said harshly. 'Your gratitude is overwhelming.'

'You want gratitude too?' Lindsay mocked angrily. 'As I remember you, the price tag on your help is high enough without any value added tax of that sort.'

He didn't like that remark; the hard-boned face tightened and a dark red stain washed through the brown skin.

'Don't push me, Lindsay, I might hit back, and you wouldn't like that, believe me.'

'I'm not afraid of you!' Lindsay threw at him, shaking with temper. She was lying, she was afraid of him, she was terrified of what would happen to Stephen and his firm if Daniel Randall decided to take an interest in it. Daniel enjoyed acquiring other firms, streamlining them into profitability through ruthless asset-stripping and what he called rationalisation, which meant in practice that he cut man-power and a lot of people lost their jobs. It was undeniable that the firms usually seemed to make more money afterwards, but Lindsay had been appalled by what she saw of her husband's cold-blooded, hard-headed business techniques. It had all fitted the other things she had learnt about him! Daniel was merciless in the pursuit of his own way.

Daniel took a step towards her and she shrank back against the couch cushions; her skin prickling with nerves as she suddenly became aware that they were quite alone down here and that all around them the house was silent.

'I thought you weren't afraid of me?' Daniel asked in dry menace, watching her restless eyes as she looked towards the door. 'What's the matter, Lindsay? Not quite as brave as you thought you were?'

'I just don't like being loomed over, that's all,' she said sulkily, looking back at him, and he smiled in a fashion which sent waves of heat up her body.

'I'd better sit down, then, hadn't I?'

She realised her mistake at once, but it was too late; he had sat down next to her, that long, lean thigh touching her, his body turned towards her, his eyes travelling in lazy speculation from her flushed face downwards over her white silk blouse and pleated skirt to her long, shapely legs. His gaze came back to her face at last, after he had reduced her to a seething cauldron of fury and resentment over the way he was inspecting her, but her open rage merely made him laugh.

'Aren't I allowed to look? You're still stunning, but I'm sure your boy-friend tells you that.'

'Boy-friend?' she repeated, startled, staring into his watchful eyes.

'The guy who left just as I arrived—I saw him getting into his car after a long kiss. Is it serious? Planning to marry him?'

'Mind your own business, what's it got to do with you?'

'Just curious,' Daniel said with a casual shrug. 'What's his name? Do I know him?'

'Not as far as I know. His name is Aston Hill.'

'It's what?' he asked laughing, and her flush deepened resentfully.

'What's funny about that? I like his name, and I like him, too; Aston's a wonderful man.'

'I'm sure he is,' agreed Daniel and she heard the bland, mocking note in his voice and glared at him.

'He is!'

'Did I deny it?'

'You were making fun of him, don't think I

didn't hear you. I'll tell you this—he's worth ten of you.'

'In what way?' he asked in all apparent soberness, but the glint in the grey eyes betrayed that he was still having fun at her expense and Lindsay looked at him with bitter dislike. 'Financially or . . .'

'All you think about is money,' she muttered. 'No, he isn't as rich as you are, but . . .

'In bed?' Daniel prompted, and alarm bells went off inside her.

'I don't want to talk about Aston,' she said hurriedly. 'I'm worried about Stephen, isn't there any way we can trace him?'

'I doubt very much if Stephen is in any danger,' Daniel dismissed coolly. 'He's far too intelligent to do anything really stupid. At a guess, I'd say he's gone away to think things out and he'll be back in a day or two. If he's been under some heavy pressure lately he could have felt that life was just too much to cope with, he had to get away by himself. He might even have felt resentful because nobody seemed to realise the sort of load he was carrying. That may be why he didn't have any message for Alice. Someone who's used up all their energy gets into a burnt-out state where they want to hit back at the people around them for not noticing what was happening to them.' He gave her a hard glance, his eyes hostile. 'Men are human beings, you know.'

'Some may be,' Lindsay muttered, then her pulses leapt with alarm as Daniel's body swung sideways, his arm going across her to fence her into the corner of the couch and his face suddenly only inches away from hers.

'Don't touch me!' The panic-stricken words escaped before she could stop them and she saw his smile harden on his mouth.

'If you wave a red rag at a bull you must expect him to charge,' he told her, his grey eyes sliding down over her, insolence in them, as though he could see through the formal clothes to the warm flesh beneath. 'That remark was deliberate provocation and you know it—I'm a human being and I can prove it.' Before she could stop him his hand was touching her breast, shaping the silken roundedness in the curved cup of palm and fingers, while he watched her intently, his other hand taking hold of her wrist in an iron grip and pulling her hand towards his shirt. He held her hand against his chest, still staring into her nervously flickering eyes.

'Feel my heart,' he said softly. 'Hear it beating? I'm flesh and blood, Lindsay, and when I touch you, every nerve cell in my body knows it.'

'Get your hands off me,' she began unsteadily, and the words were smothered as his mouth came down on hers, parting her lips with crushing force; a fierce demand which almost amounted to cruelty because it did not care if it hurt her or not, his mouth hard and insistent.

The hand touching her body moved sideways, she felt the long fingers opening her blouse, and tried to struggle free, her hands pushing at his shoulders, hitting him, thrusting at him while she writhed and fought to get away. His hand slid inside, the fingers cool on her skin, and she caught her breath shuddering, as she felt him touch her naked breast. Wild tremors ran through her, she was trembling with shock, her body arching in bitter tension. A great part of her anger was with herself because she couldn't disguise from her own mind that her body was alight with excitement at what he was doing to it; fire flashed along her nerves, her flesh was melting, and she knew that Daniel was unlikely to miss the telltale signs that betrayed her.

Desperately dragging herself back from the edge of surrender, she deliberately ran her nails into his neck and felt him jerk back in pain.

'You little fool,' he muttered, sitting up. His face was flushed and hard. He put a hand to his neck and looked at his fingertips as he took it away again. A faint smear of blood showed on his skin.

'You've made me bleed!' he exclaimed, sounding shocked. 'Look at your claw-marks, you vicious little cat!'

'I told you to leave me alone.' Lindsay got to her feet, slightly unsteady as she moved; her head spinning, the blood beating in her ears. 'I think you'd better go,' she said in a voice made raw by the wave of misery which had swept up inside her. Her body was aching with unsatisfied desire, and she hated him for having made her feel like this, she wanted him to go now before she broke down in tears. It was so long since she had felt his hands touching her, her flesh had seemed to dissolve in the furnace-like heat of her emotions.

'I'm staying here tonight,' he muttered, and she stiffened.

'Oh, no, you're not!' Did he really think she would let him stay the night? She moved backwards, watching him with nervous, frightened eyes that spat green fire in defiance, and Daniel looked back at her, his mouth crooked in sardonic mockery.

CHAPTER THREE

'DON'T be stupid, Lindsay,' he said with an impatient smile that she found infuriating. 'You need sleep as much as Alice does, but there ought to be someone awake in case something happens— I'll stay down here on the couch. I can go without sleep for days if I have to, you should remember that.' She did, of course; Daniel could work through the night and still get up at the crack of dawn looking as bright as a daisy, she had often marvelled at that ability to go without sleep. If he felt tired he could catnap in a chair for half an hour; she had seen him switch himself off like a machine, close his eyes and be asleep within seconds, to wake up bright-eyed and bushy-tailed, ready to cope with whatever emergency was needing his attention.

'It's very kind of you,' she said hesitantly, and he gave her one of his sardonic glances.

'So gracious!'

'I meant it!'

'But it hurt to say it,' he drawled.

'If I sound surprised it's because kindness isn't something I expect from you.' She ran a shaky hand through her tumbled red-gold hair, sighing.

Daniel watched her, his face calm now. 'You look like death—I suggest we discuss your distorted view of my character in the morning when you've had some sleep and can talk rationally.'

'I'm perfectly rational now.' Lindsay said, smothering a yawn, and his mouth twisted.

'That,' he said slowly, 'is a matter of opinion.'

She opened her mouth to argue, then closed it. 'I'll get you some blankets and a pillow.' He was quite right, she was too tired to talk clearly, the emotional onslaught of the last few hours had shredded her nerves and left her feeling like someone who has just been in an accident. Anxiety and tension were killing, you couldn't switch them off for long enough to restore your equilibrium, and this evening she had had a series of mental shocks which she certainly couldn't have anticipated. It seemed an eternity since she had stepped into the shower with nothing on her mind but the prospect of a lively date with Aston at the theatre, she hadn't had any premonition of what was about to hit her.

She quietly went upstairs to the bathroom airing cupboard, found some blankets and a pillow on the top shelf and took them down to Daniel, who was looking along the bookshelves that filled the alcoves on each side of the fireplace. Lindsay was moving so softly that he hadn't heard her come back; she stood there, her arms full, staring at him. In the lamplight his black hair shone like polished jet, the ends of it tapering in to his brown nape, brushing his collar as he bent forward to pull out a book. He straightened again, his movement supple, the muscled elegance of a tiger rippling beneath his tailored suit. Her breath caught and Daniel turned his head quickly.

Lindsay pulled herself together and came into the room. She dropped her burden on the couch. 'Will two blankets be enough?'

'More than adequate.' He moved towards her and she felt her nerves prickling, and hurriedly walked back to the door before he glimpsed anything of what she was feeling. 'Goodnight, then, you'll wake me if anything happens.'

She heard his soft laughter as she closed the door and was furious with herself for fleeing like a routed army. She might have known that it would be a dead give-away—Daniel Randall didn't miss a thing; she should have stood her ground and tried to look as cool as a cucumber. The very last thing she wanted was for him to guess how she felt about having him around. Their marriage was over, thank heavens, and it had cost her enough to cut herself free from him the first time around, she didn't want to get involved with him again. She had that much sense, now. She hadn't had any when she first met him, she had been too young.

It had been one of the malicious jokes of fate that she had met him in the first place—she had been nineteen, working in London as a junior secretary in a merchant bank, sharing a flat with two other girls from the bank and living as cheaply as possible on her tiny salary. Each Saturday morning, one of the secretarial staff had to come in to work to open the mail and deal with routine enquiries which couldn't wait until Monday. The girls worked a rota for this duty, so that it was only around six times a year that each one to give up her Saturday morning.

The second time Lindsay had to do it, one of the directors came into her little office and asked her to take some urgent dictation. Daniel had been with him and had wandered around the room with his hands in his pockets while the other man dictated. Lindsay had held her head down, nervously concentrating on her shorthand, but she had been very much aware of Daniel. She had never seen anyone like him, the men who worked at the bank were usually pretty boring, either stuffed shirts without two words to say for themselves or shy young men who stared at her and stammered over their dictation. Daniel had seemed like someone from another planet; she had been stunned by his electric sexuality, the masculinity of that strong face and powerful body. He wore the same dark suit and striped business shirt as the other men, but he wore his clothes with a casual panache which made them seem very different, and the way he moved somehow made it impossible not to be aware of the male body underneath the clothes. Lindsay had found herself trembling every time he came near her, she kept stealing looks at him from under her lowered lashes. He hadn't seemed to be looking at her most of the time, but once their eyes had met and Daniel had given her a quick, amused, aware smile, sending a wave of bright pink flowing up her face. She had felt so obvious, he must have realised she couldn't keep her eyes off him, and he was laughing at her. After that she had kept her eyes firmly riveted on the shorthand pad.

When she left the bank at noon to walk to her

nearest tube station she had found Daniel waiting outside in a red sports car. Lindsay hadn't noticed him at first, she had been about to walk past without a glance when he leaned over, opening the passenger door, and smiled at her. Halting in surprise, she had come over to the car, imagining that he was going to ask her some question about the work she had done that morning. Questions had flashed through her mind: had she made a mistake when she typed those letters?

'Can I give you a lift?' Daniel had asked instead, and she had hesitated, wary caution in her eyes. Daniel had watched her face, reading her expression without difficulty.

'My intentions are strictly honourable,' he had teased. 'I was only going to suggest lunch, seduction isn't on the agenda.'

She had blushed, then hated herself. He must think her so gauche and unsophisticated, she had thought, and with as casual a smile as she could manage she had got into his car, saying: 'Lunch would be fun.' Daniel had given her a smile that glinted with humour at the airy tone, and she had blushed again.

'You look like a poppy,' he had said, touching her cheek with one finger, and she had jumped about six foot in the air.

It all seemed a hundred years ago now, she had been so young and she hadn't had a clue how to talk to him. He had had a walk-over with her, one smile and she had been on her knees at his feet, amazed that anyone so godlike should want to take her out.

It was only after they were married, when
Daniel was so rarely at home, always too busy to
make dinner engagements or meet her at the
theatre as they had arranged, that she began to
view their first encounter in a different light.
How many other wide-eyed little secretaries had
he picked up so easily? He had accomplished it so
smoothly, with the ease of someone who made it a
habit. A smile, a come-hither look and she had
been in his car, her heart beating like a drum and
her senses wildly aware of every movement he
made.

Daniel had kissed her on their first date; on
their second he had taken her out to dinner and
afterwards they had sat in his car for what had
seemed eternity, the expert caresses he was giving
her turning her blood to fire. Now she had no
doubt that if she had been a different sort of girl,
she would have been in bed with him that night,
but Daniel had come up against a barrier he,
perhaps, hadn't expected. Lindsay had never
been to bed with a man in her life, she had pulled
back in panic when she realised where they were
heading.

'No, don't—I'm sorry, I can't, I've never . . .'
Her incoherent stammering had seemed to amuse
him. He had looked into her flushed face, brows
lifted, then he had smiled and run a long, gentle
finger over the trembling curve of her mouth.

'Don't get into a state, honey, I'm not going
to turn nasty, you can stop shaking in your
shoes.'

'I'm sorry,' she had said, feeling a failure,
afraid that he would lose interest in her if she

refused, yet unable to relax and let it happen. She had never thought of herself as inhibited, but her mind obstinately refused to lift that invisible barrier; she went stiff from head to foot every time she thought about it.

'Don't apologise,' he had said, and there had been a faint snap in his voice then, he had frowned angrily, sitting up.

For a minute they had sat in silence in the car, not looking at each other, and Lindsay had heard the roughened drag of his breathing, betraying his frustration, tearing at her nerves and the nagging frustration she felt herself. She had hated herself, she had desperately wanted to turn to him and say: 'Yes, please, I want to . . .' But she couldn't, her tongue seemed to have turned to wood in her mouth, she could barely swallow. The dry heat behind her eyes had become tears which stole down her face, she put up a hand to brush them away and Daniel turned his head, catching the gesture.

'Oh, hell,' he had muttered, seeing the wetness on her cheeks, 'Lindsay, you baby . . .'

There had been impatience, tenderness, exasperation in his voice, but he had put out an arm to gather her against him and his hand had pushed her head down on to his chest, his long fingers stroking her hair, ruffling it, rubbing her scalp as though she was a nervous animal he was trying to calm. Lindsay had burrowed into him, muffling a little sob, and he had put his face down on her hair.

'If I'm not careful I'm going to fall in love with you,' he had whispered, and she had closed her eyes, her body melting with happiness, hearing his heart beating beneath her cheek.

During one of their bitter rows later, she had turned on him and asked angrily: 'If you feel like that about me, why did you marry me?' and Daniel had said in barbed mockery: 'I couldn't see any other way of getting you into bed, you frigid little tease.'

It had been an admission she never forgot—if she hadn't refused to sleep with him from the start, he would never have married her, and it had taken him six months to make up his mind then, he had kept up the pressure mercilessly until he finally conceded defeat, and asked her to marry him. If Lindsay had planned the whole thing as a cool campaign she couldn't have been more successful, but she hadn't had any plan, she had merely been unable to break through that inhibition which her unconscious had had buried within it. When she first met him she hadn't even been aware of her own sexual inhibitions, she had never wanted to make love with anyone before, and if she did ever daydream about it, she had somehow pictured love as something which would happen naturally. Her imagination had not wandered beyond kisses and caresses, ending mistily, in delight, but a delight Lindsay had never looked at too closely.

She wasn't so innocent that she didn't know how men and women make love, but it was one thing to have a vague idea of the physical realities of the sexual act and quite another, she found, to bring yourself to the point of surrender that first time, and once she had said no to Daniel she found herself unable to say yes, the original inhibition had been joined by another, equally baffling to her. She had become too selfconscious about it, she was too nervous and she wanted him too much.

Looking back at herself across the years of her marriage and divorce, the painful growing years when she discovered her own identity as a woman and shed the shy uncertainties of adolescence, she felt angry and resentful now, she was very sorry for that blushing girl who could neither bring herself to say yes nor find the courage to walk away from Daniel, until he had inflicted on her wounds that still hadn't fully healed.

She went softly into the spare bedroom next to the one used by the two children, hearing their regular breathing faintly as she paused to listen for it. There wasn't a sound from Alice's room, presumably she was fast asleep too. Lindsay sighed, closing her bedroom door. Where was Stephen? Why hadn't he rung, or at least sent a telegram to ease Alice's mind? Was Daniel right when he said that Stephen was a bad case of burn-out and wanted to make Alice suffer because she hadn't even been aware of his anxieties? Undressing and slipping into bed in her white nylon slip, she switched off the light and lay on her back, her arms crossed behind her head, staring at the dark ceiling, thinking about her brother for a long time until she finally fell asleep.

She slept so deeply that she didn't hear a sound when someone opened the door and came over to the bed. It wasn't until a finger stroked her cheek that her lids flickered upwards and her eyes blinked in the morning sunlight, staring straight into Daniel's grey eyes and coming awake with speed.

'I brought you some tea and toast,' he said, those dark brows raised in wry comment on her immediately wary expression.

She must have slept restlessly, she had flung off the bedclothes during the night, and she felt him look at her bare shoulders, the half-revealed breasts under the transparent nylon slip, the soft pink flesh only too visible to him. Hurriedly she dragged the sheet around her and sat up, wrapped in a sort of toga, to drink the tea and nibble the toast while Daniel lounged on the edge of the bed and watched her.

'No news yet?' she asked, and he shook his head.

'Your reporter friend sat outside all night in his car, I think. At any rate, he's there this morning, but he hasn't tried to get near the house with my men outside.'

'Have they been there all night?'

'All night,' he agreed. 'Two more will relieve them any minute, I gather.'

'I should think they could do with some tea and toast, too, after standing around all night.'

'They sat in their car on the drive, taking turns to stay awake and on watch,' Daniel told her. 'And they've had some tea. They had sandwiches with them—they're used to this sort of work, they came prepared.'

'Like the Boy Scouts,' Lindsay remarked, finishing her toast. 'Is Alice up?'

He shook his head. 'I gave the children their breakfast at seven o'clock—they wake up early. I heard them squeaking and went in there, they seemed surprised to see a strange man, but luckily they didn't make much noise.'

Lindsay was taken aback. 'You fed them and got them up? All by yourself?'

He gave her a derisive look. 'It wasn't that difficult—women make too much fuss about looking after kids. The boy told me where to find their clothes, he dressed himself more or less while I dressed his sister, then I carried her downstairs and he told me they both wanted rusks in warm milk. They seemed quite happy with them.'

'Where are they now?' Lindsay had visions of Matt electrocuting himself by sticking his finger into the wall points, or Vicky eating one of her shoes, something Alice was always worrying about. Vicky had a habit of putting everything into her mouth, and Alice permanently fretted in case her baby died a sudden death by accident. Children, she often said to Lindsay, seem to be fascinated by fatal objects, you have to watch them twenty-four hours a day.

'I belted them both into high-chairs in the sitting-room and left them staring at the test card on the TV.' Daniel seemed pleased with his achievements as a baby-sitter, he grinned at her in self-congratulation.

'That must be exciting for them,' commented Lindsay, on the point of getting out of the bed to go and rescue the poor children when she realised she was practically naked under her sheet.

Flushing, she said: 'I want to get dressed—would you mind?'

'Not at all.' Daniel said smoothly, settling himself more comfortably on the bed. 'Carry on, don't worry about me.'

Eyeing him with distaste, she said: 'Oh, but I do worry about you—I'm not getting dressed in front of you, so go away.'

'You know your problem?' Daniel asked slowly uncoiling himself with reluctance.

'Yes, it's standing in front of me and it's six foot tall.'

'Apart from me,' he said, moving to the door. 'Your trouble is, you're no fun any more. You've lost your sense of humour.'

'I didn't lose it, I still laugh at you,' she assured him from behind her veil of sheeting. 'All the time, believe me.'

He gave her a look which was not amused and went out. Lindsay waited until she heard him going down the stairs, then she slid out of the bed and picked up her clothes. Opening the door, she risked a quick dash to the bathroom, showered rapidly and got dressed. When she had brushed her hair and applied a little make-up she went downstairs to say hallo to Matt and Vicky, who were, as Daniel had told her, deeply engrossed in the test card, but were also playing with some toys arranged on the trays of their high-chairs. At the sight of her, Vicky threw a yellow wooden brick at her, beaming, and Matt gravely offered her one of his miniature cars.

Lindsay gave them both a kiss. 'Having a good time?'

'Mumma get up,' said Vicky, hurling some more bricks at her while she displayed all her pearly teeth in a wide grin. 'Up, up, Mumma get up, bad Mumma.'

'We had rusks,' Matt announced. 'And black-currant juice and banana, and Vicky ate mine, she ate my banana.' He looked at Lindsay with his father's eyes and she kissed his nose.

'Too bad, darling, I'll get you another banana.'

'I don't like bananas,' he said. 'Vicky ate mine.'

'Oh, I see, it was a friendly arrangement, was it?' He looked vague. 'Vicky ate my banana.'

'Don't let it weigh on your mind,' Lindsay advised. 'If you don't like bananas, that's okay by me.'

Daniel came in and grinned at her. 'I'm relieved to discover other people have the same inconsequential conversations with them that I had—I thought it was me, I just wasn't on their wavelength.'

'Vicky ate my banana,' Matt told him.

'He's obsessed with that damned banana,' Daniel said to her. 'I offered him another one and he refused.'

'He doesn't like them, but he feels guilty about it,' Lindsay explained, deciphering Matt's worried expression.

'Why on earth should he?'

'I expect Alice feels he ought to like them, she does tend to do things by the book, and babies are supposed to like bananas.'

Daniel studied Matt, who was pushing one of his toys cars backwards and forwards. 'If she isn't careful, he'll grow up with a banana phobia.'

'He worries,' said Lindsay, and frowned, reminded of Stephen—yes, Matt was just like his father; why had she never seen it so clearly before? There was that little nervous frown, the sober anxious look of the eyes, the smile which was too eager to please, the awareness of what was expected of him and the desire to be approved of by everyone. 'Poor Stephen,' she said, mostly to herself, and Daniel looked at her sharply.

'I thought his name was Matt.'

'It is,' said Lindsay, stiffening as she heard movements on the stairs. The door was pushed open and Alice came in, smiling as the two children leapt about and shouted to her. She looked much better, Lindsay thought, watching as she kissed them both. This morning she had more colour, some of the drawn tension had left her small face and she was wearing a very pretty coral linen dress which flattered her slender figure. The curly red-brown hair had been brushed until it gleamed and she was wearing make-up, Lindsay noted. A woman who is very depressed forgets to look at herself in mirrors, she doesn't bother to do her hair or make-up, she no longer cares what she looks like. Alice was obviously feeling less miserable after her long sleep.

'Any news?' she asked Lindsay a second later, and in her brown eyes Lindsay saw anxiety. Shaking her head, Lindsay admitted there was none.

'Daniel talked to Mr Datchet last night, though,' she said before Alice's spirits could sink too low. 'Stephen owes the bank a lot of money, it seems, and Mr Datchet said he was very worried about it. Daniel thinks maybe Stephen has gone off to try to raise a loan from somewhere.'

Alice sat down with Vicky on her lap. 'Oh,' was all she could say.

'So you see it was money, after all.' At least it wasn't another woman, Lindsay thought, but carefully did not put into words. Alice could do her own thinking, and, from the look of her, that was just what she was doing, both arms clasped around the little girl's wriggling body in the vivid green dungarees and striped T-shirt, which made her look like an elf. Alice was holding Vicky far too tightly as though she needed the comfort of that small, plump, warm body, and Vicky was squawking in protest.

Daniel had leaned there, listening and watching but saying nothing. He wasn't wearing a jacket or tie, his white shirt was open at the collar; he looked casually and maddeningly good-looking, and as Lindsay irritably glanced his way he winked at her, which made her prickle with resentment.

'Mr Datchet is coming over here at ten,' he intervened a second later. 'He's bringing the firm's account books. I thought they might give us a clearer picture of what's wrong. I may be able to help Stephen, he should have contacted me long ago.'

Alice looked round, sighing. 'He's much too proud, you're the last person he would ask for help.' She flushed at Daniel's expression and hurriedly added: 'Don't be offended, I didn't mean . . . it's just that Stephen would feel that— the divorce, I mean, Lindsay isn't your wife any more and it would be embarrassing for both of you. Stephen wouldn't have wanted to put you in an awkward position by asking for a favour.'

'I could always have said no,' Daniel said drily.

'He was perfectly well aware of that,' snapped Lindsay, glaring at him. 'That's obvious, but it would still have been embarrassing to have to ask—Stephen isn't the type to trade on family loyalty, he would much rather ask a bank. If they said no, neither side need feel embarrassed, it would just be business, but if he had asked you and you had said no, Stephen would have felt two feet high.'

Alice nodded. 'Lindsay's right.'

'Well, that's a first,' Daniel drawled, and got a dagger-bright smile from Lindsay.

Before she could say what was hovering on the tip of her tongue, the doorbell went, and Daniel straightened.

'I'll go, it may be Mr Datchet,' he said, going out.

'Perhaps Stephen will ring today,' said Alice, putting Vicky back into her high-chair. 'If he's only worried about money . . .'

'I told you it wasn't another woman—Stephen loves you,' Lindsay said in a low voice. 'He's probably worried sick about telling you about the bank loan.'

'How could he be so stupid?' Alice broke off as the door opened again and Daniel walked into the room, bringing with him a distinctly dangerous air of menace and Aston Hill wearing a grey suit, a pale blue shirt and a wryly amused expression.

'Your boy-friend,' Daniel said acidly, hurling the words at Lindsay as if he hoped they would knock her head off with the force of their arrival.

'Hallo, darling,' said Aston, just as deliberately, with the smile of one determined to enjoy a difficult situation just for the hell of it.

Vicky decided she liked the look of Aston, and held out her arms to him lovingly. 'Uncle,' she said, and Lindsay could have killed her. She had such a small vocabulary, why couldn't she have chosen one of her other words?

Playing up to her, Aston advanced and gave her a kiss on her cheek. 'Hallo, sweetheart, you look gorgeous as usual.' He had only set eyes on Vicky once or twice before, he was being difficult, but Daniel deserved it, acting as though Aston was an interloper.

'I came round right away,' Aston said. 'I gather Stephen hasn't got in touch with you yet?'

Alice tried to smile, it was not a success, her lips trembled too much. 'No.'

'Then I've got news for you,' Aston told her. 'He rang me an hour ago, he's quite safe, so you can stop worrying.'

CHAPTER FOUR

'HE rang *you*?' Alice's voice went up several octaves and she flushed angrily. 'Stephen rang you, not me? Why? What did he say to you?'

'He wasn't very coherent,' Aston explained. 'He was upset . . .'

'Upset? *He's* upset? What does he think I am? He vanishes without a word of explanation, stays away for hours and then rings a perfect stranger?' She looked at Aston, shrugging. 'Oh, I'm sorry, I didn't mean to sound rude, but he hardly knows you. I'm his wife, how can he do this to me? Where is he?'

'He's staying at a country pub, he didn't say where. It seems he couldn't face coming home, so he drove and drove until he was tired, then he stopped at this pub for a drink and ended up staying the night.'

'Why didn't he come home next day?' Alice was walking about the room restlessly, her hands clenched, spots of burning colour in her cheeks.

'He woke up with a hangover, a blinding headache. He felt sick, so he stayed in bed all morning. By the time he had got over that, he didn't know what to say to you. He tried to ring Lindsay last night, but she wasn't answering her phone, of course, she was here. So he rang me this morning.'

Alice faced him belligerently, chin up. 'And

why hasn't he rung me? He could talk to you but not to me—how am I supposed to feel about that?'

Lindsay glanced at the children, who were very quiet, studiously playing with their toys and hoping not to be noticed. 'What we need is some coffee,' she said brightly. 'I'll make some. Matt can help me—come on, Matt.' She scooped up Vicky under one arm and headed for the door; this conversation was not one which the two children should hear. They might not entirely understand what was being said, but they would be picking up far too much from their mother's angry excitement and the way she talked about their father.

Alice didn't even seem to notice, she was too distressed. 'If he's in trouble I'm the one he should be talking to, not a stranger,' she protested to Aston, who made conciliating noises.

'I'm sure he'll ring you any minute . . .'

Lindsay closed the door on the rest of that sentence and went into the kitchen with the children. Before she made the coffee she got them dressed in their identical little knitted jackets and put them both into the garden to play in their sandpit. It was a warm morning, the sky was blue and cloudless, there was a slight breeze blowing through the trees. Lindsay stood for a moment, watching Matt digging with a plastic spade while Vicky sat on the sand and picked up handfuls that trickled through her plump pink fingers in a silvery shower. Stephen had built the sandpit for them. Lindsay sighed and went back into the house.

She found Daniel in the kitchen, spooning ground coffee into the percolater. He looked up. 'Will they be okay out there on their own?'

'Of course.' She took the percolater from him and plugged it into the wall point, pretending not to be aware of his narrow-eyed stare.

'Odd that Stephen should ring Hill and nobody else,' Daniel observed. 'Are they close friends?'

'They get on well.' Lindsay got out the cups. The sun was streaming through the window, giving the small room a much happier look this morning, or was that merely because she saw it with different eyes now that she knew her brother was safe?

'Is Hill in the same business?' Daniel asked, leaning back against a formica-topped cabinet, his arms folded across his chest.

'He has some shops; he sells electrical equipment, so I suppose in a sense he is in the same business as Stephen.'

'So he might be in a position to help Stephen out of trouble?'

She looked round at him. 'How should I know? You'd have to ask them, I'm not involved in Stephen's business.'

'Your sister-in-law said something about Stephen being reluctant to ask for help from me because we were divorced,' Daniel drawled.

'I'm sure she's right, Stephen's very proud.'

'So why would he ask Hill for help? Unless he thinks that any day now Hill's going to be his brother-in-law?'

Lindsay heard the terse note in the voice and felt herself flushing. She didn't answer, and luckily the coffee started bubbling right then and she could make a big show of being too busy to say anything, switching off the percolater and unplugging it from the wall. Daniel moved softly, she didn't hear him until he was right behind her, and his voice made her jump when it came so close he was almost whispering into her ear.

'No comment?'

'None of your business,' Lindsay retorted, checking the tray to make sure she had everything: cups, sugar, coffee pot, milk. She kept her eyes down, her back towards him, trying not to be aware of his close proximity.

'You're not in love with Hill!' Daniel sounded self-satisfied, his voice purring, and her temper began to rise like mercury in an exploding thermometer.

'Who says?'

'I do,' he told her in maddening amusement.

'What you know about love could be written on a postage stamp,' Lindsay muttered in an impeded voice, trying not to lose control. She was too old to slap his face, she wasn't going to descend to that level, although no doubt he'd like that, it would give him an excuse to use his own hands in a very different way. She was going to keep calm, whatever his provocation.

'You can't hide love, I don't have to be an expert on the subject to know that,' Daniel drawled, smiling. She heard the smile in his voice and grew angrier. What was so funny? 'And I saw how you looked at Hill,' he added, giving the remark an intonation which she disliked intensely.

'Maybe I'm not as obvious as you think I am,' she returned with a bite, wishing she dared turn and hit him, because there was an element of truth in what he had said and to herself she couldn't deny it. She liked Aston very much, she admired and respected him, but she couldn't pretend she was head over heels in love with him, he didn't make her pulse beat faster, he didn't set her body on fire, but then she had outgrown that sort of love, it didn't last, and she wanted something more real, more permanent, which Aston *could* give her. Going up in flames is all very well, but what happens when the fire goes out and all that's left is charcoal? She never again wanted to end up in charred, blackened little pieces.

'Did I say you were obvious?' Daniel took hold of her elbows and spun her round to face him, so fast she didn't have time to break away. Angrily, she glared up at him, which was a mistake, because there was a wicked mockery in those silvery eyes, and more than that, an intention which she glimpsed too late, his gaze drifting downwards to her mouth just a second before his head swooped down. 'Only to me,' he whispered as his lips parted her own.

Had he used brutal force she would have struggled violently, hit him, fought free somehow, but Daniel was not making the mistake of using force this time, and he took her off guard by his devious, unscrupulous tactics, enlisting her own body as an ally against her. His mouth coaxed and incited, moving with slow, warm sensuality, the tip of his tongue flicking between her trembling lips, and Lindsay felt perspiration spring out on her forehead, she couldn't keep her eyes open. The way he was kissing her made her dizzy, she had to cling to him to stay upright as her head spun. She didn't want to feel like that again; the intensity of her passion for him had almost destroyed her once before, she had told herself she was free of him now, he couldn't get to her again, but where Daniel Randall was concerned she seemed to be schizophrenic, split into two. Torn between love and hate, between bitter contempt and a fierce compulsion, her body was dissolving in heated excitement as his hands touched her with that lingering seduction, one of them moving up and down her back while the other softly stroked her throat, her shoulders, her breasts. Her hands went up jerkily to catch his head, hold it, her fingers in his black hair, she swayed closer, wanting to melt into him, and remembered that that was how it had been, that was what love meant, this nagging desire to merge with him, hold him inside her and never let him go.

Daniel moved, breathing harshly, and she was separate from him again, their bodies parted, their mouths disentangled. She felt cold and desolate, she shuddered as she pushed him even farther away, almost too dazed to realise that they were in Alice's kitchen in the sunshine with the fragrance of fresh coffee filling the air. Time had seemed to stop, she had moved outside herself into Daniel, existing in a black velvet world of hands and lips and smothering, sweet sensations. It hurt to come back to reality.

She couldn't bring herself to speak. Trembling and darkly flushed, she picked up the tray of coffee and walked unsteadily towards the door.

'That's it, run away from it,' Daniel said behind her, but she pretended not to have heard, she kept on going with her eyes fixed on nothing, the cups on the tray rattling as her hands shook. What had just happened had not come as any real surprise to her; she had stayed away from him just because he could do that to her. The physical chemistry between them was explosive, Lindsay couldn't deny that, she had always known that he could reach her on that level. Daniel was a male animal with powerful sexual magnetism, Lindsay couldn't deny that, either, but neither could she forget that other women felt his attraction. Daniel wasn't a man who belonged to anyone, Lindsay had wasted too much of her life burning with jealousy because he was turning those mocking grey eyes on another woman.

How many evenings had she spent alone during their marriage, wondering who he was with? How many parties had she gone to with him only to see him dancing with someone else and ache with misery over the way he was smiling down at his partner? He was ruthless in business, she hadn't expected him to be so ruthless in his private life; she had thought he was hers, but she had discovered just how wrong she was—Daniel Randall belonged to himself. Lindsay's dazed incredulity when he first told her he loved her and asked her to marry him had become gradually a bitter disenchantment. Her first uneasy suspicions had hardened into certainties, she had become sure that Daniel had only married her because he couldn't seduce her, but once he had got what he wanted he had gone back to his old way of life. Her jealousy began to corrode her every waking moment, she couldn't bear the unremitting pain, she had had to get away from him.

She shouldn't have let him get so close to her just now, she would be crazy if she walked back into that trap. However temptingly baited, it would end the way it had ended before, with her getting badly hurt.

In the sitting-room, she found Alice walking round and round, her arms clasping her shoulders, a hard flush on her cheeks. 'I'll kill him,' she was saying. 'I'll kill him.'

Aston glanced towards the door as Lindsay came in and winked at her surreptitiously. To Alice he said: 'He was worried about you.'

'Funny way of showing it!' Alice would not be placated.

Lindsay put down the tray. 'Coffee,' she said. 'Come on, Alice, sit down and relax.'

'Relax? I'm on wires, I couldn't sit down.' She kept on walking, scowling.

'We ought to tell the police that Stephen's okay,' Lindsay said to Aston as she poured him coffee.

Alice stopped dead. 'I'd forgotten them— whatever will they think? I feel such a fool—there was I ringing the police, crying my eyes out, and all the time he was sleeping off a hangover!'

'Drink your coffee,' said Lindsay, handing her

a cup. 'I'll ring the police and explain, I'm sure they'll understand.'

They did; Lindsay heard the amusement in the duty sergeant's voice. 'Thought it might be something like that,' he said. 'Happens all the time.' I told you so, his voice silently breathed. Far from being angry at the waste of police time he was pleased with himself for having been right.

'I'm sorry to have troubled you over nothing,' Lindsay said, all the same.

'No trouble, miss, that's what we're here for. Very glad the gentleman turned up safe and sound.' He could hardly wait to ring off and tell his friends he had guessed right. Lindsay put down the phone, grimacing.

As she turned round, Aston joined her. 'I've got a vital appointment this morning. I must be off,' he said, smiling at her, and she linked her arms around his neck, leaning towards him.

'Did I say how grateful I am? It was good of you to come over to give Alice the news, you're a darling.' She kissed him lightly and Aston's hands closed on her waist, drawing her nearer. His mouth came down with warm insistence on her own and Lindsay swayed against him, kissing him back.

A moment later, Aston murmured: 'What's Randall doing here? Didn't he go out of your life a long time ago?' The question made Lindsay stiffen.

She leaned back to look up at him. 'A reporter rang him and told him Stephen was missing, so he came round to find out what was going on.'

'This morning?' Aston asked, and her eyes flicked down, she felt herself flush. Before she could think of a way of answering that awkward question, he said drily: 'He looks very much at home here, and who are the two gorillas out on the drive? They made me prove my identity before they would let me near the front door, and even then they hung around until Randall had spoken to me. I picked up that they came from his zoo and took their orders from him.'

'The press kept ringing the door bell. Daniel felt we needed protection.'

'How long have they been out there?'

'All night,' said Lindsay, and then her eyes met Aston's and she sighed.

'Which means so has he,' Aston thought aloud.

'Yes, he arrived just after you left last night.' Lindsay felt she ought to be apologising, Aston made her feel guilty, as though she had invited Daniel here.

'And stayed all night.' Aston's air of good humour was not so much in evidence at this moment, his jaw had hardened, he was frowning and she read accusation in his eyes.

'On the couch downstairs!' Lindsay knew she was very flushed, she hoped she did not look guilty.

'And where were you?'

'Upstairs,' she said crossly. 'In the spare bedroom.'

'All night?'

'All night!' she agreed, her chin up defiantly, meeting his probing stare without flinching. 'And before you ask—no, he did not make love to me last night. If he'd tried, I'd have knocked him into the middle of next week!'

Aston relaxed slightly, half-smiling. 'He seems very concerned for an ex-husband,' he said, though. 'I didn't expect to find him here.'

'He's interested in Stephen's business, if Stephen isn't careful Daniel Randall will be running his firm.' Lindsay heard the sting of bitterness in her own voice and saw Aston's eyes widen.

'Like that, is it? He isn't interested in you, then? He seemed very hostile when I told him I'd come to see you, I thought for a minute he was going to punch my face in . . .'

'Daniel's an aggressive man.'

'You mean he always talks like that?' Aston whistled softly, his face wry. 'That must be wearing to live with.'

'It is—I told you, I can't stand the sight of him.'

Aston laughed. 'I'm not too smitten myself, but then I have good reason not to be—even if he'd been charming to me, there was no way I'd have liked the guy.'

Lindsay didn't pretend not to know what he meant, she smiled up at him, shaking her head. 'You don't need to be jealous of Daniel Randall, nothing would tempt me back to him.'

Aston wound a hand into her gleaming red-gold hair, kissed her gently on the mouth. 'I hope you mean that—in case you hadn't noticed, I'm your fan for life and you're much too beautiful to be wasted on a hard case like Daniel Randall.' He opened the front door, waved a hand at her. 'Stay in touch, and don't let Randall within a foot of you.'

'I won't,' she promised, and stood at the door waving as he got into his car and drove away under the watchful gaze of Daniel's security men. Lindsay resisted the temptation to put out her tongue at them, closing the door with a slam.

Slow clapping made her spin in shock. Daniel stood at the door of the kitchen, lounging casually against the frame, derisively applauding her.

'Were you eavesdropping?' Lindsay asked angrily.

'I was a fascinated audience,' he drawled. 'Your performance was touching—such wide-eyed sincerity, you almost convinced me.'

'I meant every word!'

'And I just imagined the way you kissed me half an hour ago!' he mocked, bringing a hot wave of colour flowing up to her hairline.

'*You* kissed *me*!'

'I don't remember you struggling.'

'Your memory has never been very reliable.'

'On the contrary, my memory is infallible,' Daniel corrected with a smile which she found detestable, the crooked amusement in it brought back too many memories of her own.

'Oh, of course, it would be,' she flung back, seething. 'Infallible and omniscient, aren't you?'

'I know you rather better than you seem to know yourself,' he told her, and she turned away, shaking with temper, to go into the sitting-room. Daniel did not follow her and a moment later she heard him talking to someone in the hall. Alice went to the door, looked out and came back a second later.

'Mr Datchet,' she said dully as Lindsay eyed her enquiringly.

'You ought to see him,' Lindsay said. 'Stephen might not be too happy to come back and find that Daniel Randall has been inspecting his account books.'

'I suppose you're right.' Reluctantly, Alice left the room. Lindsay heard her voice from the hall. 'Hallo, Mr Datchet . . .'

Lindsay went to the window and looked out. The sky was clouding over, the sun had vanished behind a bank of stormy slate-blue cloud hanging low over the surrounding roof-tops, and a sudden wind was whipping the tops of trees into frothy green tangles of leaves. She decided she should bring the two children back into the house, it looked as if it might rain at any minute.

The hall was empty, and she heard Daniel's voice from a little room leading off it which Stephen used as a study and office. Lindsay walked through the kitchen and into the garden. Matt was running aimlessly around the lawn while Vicky shovelled sand into a small bucket. They both started towards her eagerly.

'It's cold,' Matt said. 'Can we come in?'

'In,' said Vicky, lifting her arms.

Lindsay hoisted her up and Matt darted past her into the house, shouting: 'Mummy, Mummy!'

When Lindsay went into the kitchen a moment later, Vicky clinging to her like a little monkey, she found Alice kneeling on the floor unbuttoning Matt's jacket.

'Your hands are frozen,' she was saying, and Matt was looking reproachfully at Lindsay.

'Auntie made us stay in the garden for hours!'

'He's almost blue!' complained Alice turning a glare on Lindsay.

'It was sunny when I put them out there, I thought they would have fun playing in their sandpit.'

'Poor baby!' crooned Alice snatching Vicky from her. 'Is she cold, then?'

'Sorry,' said Lindsay under the barrage of three pairs of accusing eyes, and slipped out of the room, feeling very guilty.

A few moments later Alice took the two children upstairs, talking cheerfully to them. Lindsay heard the sound of a vacuum cleaner in the bedrooms—Alice had decided to vent her fury with Stephen on the housework and the children were helping, Lindsay heard Vicky chattering to herself as she fetched and carried for her mother. Daniel and Mr Datchet were still in the study, their voices low. Conspiratorial? wondered Lindsay, listening at the door unashamedly. What exactly was Daniel up to in there?

It was a Saturday morning; Lindsay should have been doing her own housework in the flat, or her shopping, which she always did at weekends. After she had divorced Daniel she had had to go back to work, of course. She hadn't been able to face the idea of working in another bank, secretarial work didn't exactly enthrall her and she had had no training for any other career. For a few months she had worked for an agency, doing temp work in a variety of firms, but always keeping an eye open for a job which might be exciting. When she was sent to work for a few weeks in the publicity department of a national cosmetics firm she had enjoyed herself so much that she had jumped at the chance of working there full-time. Her first job at Vivons had been badly paid, tiring and repetitive; she had been put in charge of answering letters from the public for which a standard letter had been printed. All Lindsay did all day was to type in the name of the person to whom the letter was going, then type their name and address on the envelope After a week of this, she was almost climbing the wall, it was even more boring than working in a bank. But she had gritted her teeth and stuck it out, and after three months, which had seemed like an eternity at the time, she had been promoted to a job with more responsibility and a lot more job-satisfaction.

Now she was second in command in the public relations department, she earned more than she had ever earned before and she loved her work. She had discovered she had a flair for thinking up ideas, she had learnt how to work with the press and how to block stories which could harm the firm. She worked in a busy, lively office full of people with quick, alert minds, she was successful and self-reliant. She was no longer the unsophisticated innocent who had been bowled over by Daniel Randall's first smile, it had cost her a good deal, but she had made herself into a woman she could respect. When you despise yourself, life isn't worth living.

From learning to respect herself, she had learnt more about other people, too. She saw Daniel Randall far more clearly, for a start, and she did not trust him. She met a lot of men like him in the course of her job; opportunistic, devious men with corkscrew minds and no scruples. Lindsay was worried about his intentions towards her brother's firm. Stephen was going to be horrified when he found out that Daniel had been prying into his affairs. Why had Alice allowed Mr Datchet to show Daniel the books?

The sound of rain on the window made her look up. The weather had broken, the clouds sagged low over the roofs opposite and the pavements were dancing with great spots of rain. The two security men sat in their car staring out glumly. There was no sign of the reporter—he must have given up and gone.

Stephen still hadn't got in touch with Alice— what was the matter with him? Now that Lindsay knew he was safe, she saw his behaviour as even more out of character. Stephen had always taken his responsibilities so seriously, it wasn't like him to let Alice worry. Was he having a nervous breakdown? Something must be very wrong with him or he wouldn't be doing this. He must have been carrying an intolerable load for months without any of them noticing. They took him for granted, Stephen had always been able to cope, whatever life had thrown at him. Lindsay loved and respected her brother, she had always felt she could depend on him whenever she had problems, but now she realised that she had never wondered if he needed any help or support; he had seemed

so much in control of his life. This silence of his
was a cry for help which he hadn't been able to
put into words, she saw that now, and she was
angry with herself for not having realised
anything was wrong with him until now.

A car drew up outside the house. Lindsay
glanced at it and did a double-take, her body
stiffening. Stephen's car! She started towards the
sitting-room door. From upstairs she heard the
vacuum cleaner—Alice must have missed the
engine note. Lindsay flung open the front door
and looked out. Stephen was talking to the two
security men, a few feet away. He was wearing a
cream raincoat, his head bare, and the rain was
pelting down around him.

'Stephen!' Lindsay called, and he turned
towards her. The men stood back, watching.
Stephen slowly came up the drive, his body heavy
and slumped, his hair plastered to his skull, rain
running down his face like tears. He couldn't meet
her eyes, he looked haggard and beaten. Lindsay
ran to meet him and hugged him, trying not to cry.

Pulling him into the house, she shut the front
door on the watching security men, resenting
their curiosity.

Stephen looked up the stairs. Alice stood at the
top of them, staring down at him, her face
working. Lindsay walked into the kitchen and
shut the door; when she was alone she let her
tears escape, they stung her eyes and made her
throat ache. Poor Stephen! she thought, re-
membering his expression as he stood looking at
Alice. She had never thought she would ever see
her brother look like that.

CHAPTER FIVE

'WHAT did Stephen have to say when he realised you'd seen his firm's books?' Lindsay asked Daniel later.

He was driving her back to her flat in the slashing rain which had apparently settled in for the day, and Lindsay had to raise her voice to be heard above the clatter of the windscreen wipers and the hiss of tyres on wet roads. She would have turned down Daniel's offer of a lift if it hadn't been for the weather, but it was a long walk to the nearest tube station and she hadn't wanted to ask Stephen to take her.

Daniel glanced at her sideways, shrugging. 'He didn't have much to say about anything, did he?'

Stephen had come downstairs and gone into the study, talked to Mr Datchet for a few minutes and then walked with his accountant to the front door. Both men had been very quiet; Lindsay had got the impression Stephen was too depressed to care what happened to his firm. If Daniel's interest in his financial position bothered him, he hadn't shown it, and Lindsay had decided not to say any more to her brother than she could help. As soon as Mr Datchet had left, she had told Alice she was going, too, and Alice had been openly relieved. Obviously, she had wanted to be alone with Stephen. They had a lot to say to each other, and they didn't want a third party around, even if she was a member of the family.

'Stay out of his life,' snapped Lindsay, glaring at Daniel now. 'He can do without your brand of help.'

'Can he?' Daniel smiled without looking at her, she caught the dry movement of his mouth and fumed.

'Yes, he can!'

'Of course, you're an expert on how to salvage wrecks.'

Lindsay wasn't sure what he meant by that, but she didn't like the sound of it. 'I'm serious, Daniel!' she warned. 'Leave Stephen alone or . . .'

'Threatening me?' he mocked. 'I'm shivering in my shoes. What happens if I don't do as I'm told?' He pulled up outside her block of flats and glanced out of the window without waiting to hear her answer. 'We'll have to run for it,' he said, and Lindsay sat upright.

'We? I don't remember inviting you into my flat?'

Daniel produced an umbrella from the back of the car. He got out and opened it and Lindsay ran round to dive under its shelter. They ran up the steps, the rain beating down on the thin silk, but once she was inside the building, Lindsay stopped and gave him a frosty look.

'Thanks for the lift.'

'What are you afraid of?' Daniel asked, watching her with cool grey eyes which saw too much and had too much intelligence behind them.

'I'm not afraid of anything, I'm just tired, and I'm not in the mood for one of your barbed chats.'

'We're going to have to talk soon,' said Daniel, shaking drops of rain off the umbrella.

'We've got nothing to talk about.'

'Oh, yes, we have,' he contradicted, and there was a distant triumph in his voice, he was smiling tightly, his mouth curling up at the ends yet not parted.

Lindsay felt her stomach cave in suddenly, she grew alarmed. Why was he looking at her like that?

'About what?' she faltered, and Daniel lifted his brows, glancing around.

'I don't think this is the place for that sort of discussion.'

Lindsay turned and went up the flight of stairs, her footsteps echoing on the stone floors, and behind her she heard the sound of Daniel's following footsteps and shivered, listening to them; he somehow contrived to give the very way he walked an air of menace. She felt as if she was being hunted down, she involuntarily quickened her own pace and Daniel followed suit, his breathing calm and level while Lindsay's was far too quick and uneven.

At first she couldn't find her key and even after she'd traced it down in her handbag she couldn't get it into the lock, her fingers were too unsteady. She felt Daniel watching her and flushed, angry with herself for letting him get to her. She was playing into his hands by making a fool of herself in front of him. She pulled herself together as the front door opened, mentally scolding herself. She was not going to let Daniel undermine her.

'I'm going to make some tea—would you like some?' she asked as casually as she could manage.

'Fine,' said Daniel, walking into the sitting-room as though he owned the flat. She glared at his back but decided not to lose her temper. Shedding her jacket, she went into the kitchen to put on the kettle. She was just making the tea when she heard Daniel's voice, talking on the phone to someone. Lindsay carried the tea tray into the room as he put the phone down, turning towards her.

'Make yourself at home,' Lindsay said sarcastically, and he grinned at her.

'Thanks.' He watched her put the tray down, but as he started towards her, the phone rang again and he whirled and picked it up before Lindsay could get over there. 'Hallo?' he said, listened, then frowned, holding the phone out to her. 'Get rid of him sharpish,' he said, walking away as she lifted the receiver to her ear.

'Hallo?' she said, and Aston demanded: 'What the hell is he doing in your flat?'

'I just got back from Stephen's, Daniel drove me home,' Lindsay told him, keeping her back towards Daniel's intent figure and angrily aware that he was listening to every word she said.

'I know, I rang them—I spoke to your brother. Lindsay, I hope Randall isn't going to be around too much in future. What is he up to?'

'I don't know, I'm going to find out,' said Lindsay in a casual voice.

'Watch yourself, darling,' Aston urged, sounding anxious. 'Have dinner with me tonight? We can talk then.'

'I'd love to,' said Lindsay.

'Pick you up at seven?'

'Seven? Fine, see you then.'

'I think you're fantastic,' said Aston, and she smiled.

'Same here.' Her voice had lifted, become confident and intimate; there was something exciting about talking to Aston while Daniel listened and could only hear half the conversation. Aston blew her a kiss and she laughed.

' 'Bye, see you soon.' She would have liked to send him back a kiss, but she didn't quite dare with Daniel listening, which was ridiculous, because why should she be inhibited by his presence? She put down the phone and turned to feel a shock of alarm as she met the fixed stare of his dangerous grey eyes. Her smile withered and she flinched, then rallied. How dared he look at her like that? He had no right to resent another man's interest in her, they weren't married any more, she was a free agent.

Managing to smile brightly, she said: 'Aston just wanted to ask me out to dinner.' He needn't think she was going to hide her relationship with Aston from him, because she certainly was not going to, she had a right to a love life, as much as he did. She could be quite sure Daniel had dated other women since they broke up, why shouldn't she do the same?

'Tonight?' Daniel asked, and she nodded. 'Sleeping with him?' he asked, and her nerves jarred, she flushed.

'Mind your own business!' Then she spoilt her offended attitude by demanding crossly: 'Who are you sleeping with?'

Daniel's smile mocked her. 'Tonight? Who knows? Are you offering?'

Crimson, she snapped: 'You've got to be kidding! I'm not into masochism.' She sat down in a chair and began to pour the tea. Daniel sat down on the couch and took the cup she handed him, sipping the tea thoughtfully.

'What did you want to talk to me about?' Lindsay demanded.

'Stephen's bankrupt.' The statement was flat and cool, and Lindsay heard it with shocked incredulity.

'Bankrupt? But surely if he raises a loan to pay off the bank . . .'

'Nobody with any commercial acumen would lend that firm a brass farthing,' Daniel said brutally, and she winced. 'Stephen owes more than he owns, for the past two years he has been running at a heavy loss and he's used up all his spare capital. He'll have to sell up, even the house will have to go.'

'Oh, no!' Lindsay breathed, paling. 'Poor Alice . . .'

'The firm does have some potential,' Daniel told her. 'It will need a large influx of capital to make it viable, but with the right management it could become profitable in a few years.'

Lindsay looked at him with bitter anger. 'You, you mean?'

'I could make something of it,' he agreed coolly, watching her stormy face, then added with a shrug: 'It would hardly be worth my while, though—I wouldn't get much of a return on my time, trouble and money.'

She trembled with contempt, her green eyes shooting sparks at him. 'That's all you think about—making money!'

'Not all,' he said in a silky voice, smiling. 'I might be persuaded to make an investment in your brother's firm on the right terms.'

'What do you want? Blood?' Lindsay muttered scathingly, and he laughed.

'No. You.'

She almost dropped her cup and saucer. Slowly she put them back on to the tray, her eyes fixed on his bland face, her body rigid and chilled.

'What's that suppose to mean?'

'Don't pretend to be dumb, Lindsay, you know exactly what it means. You're even sexier than you were when I met you.' His assessing gaze moved down over her without haste and she felt her skin burn as though he was actually touching her. Her mouth went dry and a quiver of nervous reaction went through her. Daniel's eyes were undressing her, and she hated it and was excited by it all at the same time.

'You lecher! ' she burst out, her voice shaky. 'No way. You can forget that idea—I'd rather die!'

'Would you? I wonder,' he said drily, and laughed, which made her feel about two inches high.

Scrambling to her feet, she stammered: 'Get out of here before I lose my temper!'

Daniel rose and she backed, very much aware that they were alone, her hasty movement making him smile in sardonic enjoyment. He strolled towards her and she looked around for something to hit him with if he touched her, but he pushed his hands into his pockets as he halted and tilted his black head to one side, amusement in his lean face.

'I'll give you twenty-four hours to think my proposition over,' he told her as lazily as though it had been a formal business offer.

'You've had my answer. I meant it.' She had to take a deep breath before she could answer him, she was so angry.

His mouth twisted crookedly. 'It's a woman's privilege to change her mind.'

'Not this woman. My mind's made up, it has been for two years, as far as you're concerned. I don't want to know about you.'

There was a hint of cruelty about his tight smile, a brooding anger in the grey eyes. Daniel had not liked that. 'We'll see,' was all he said, though, and he walked past her without looking at her again.

She stood there, frozen on the spot, and heard him open the front door and close it with a controlled quietness which was even more menacing than that look he had just given her. Daniel Randall was a man who enjoyed getting his own way, he was ruthless and determined, and when Lindsay walked out on their marriage she had offended him bitterly. He might still find her very attractive, but she couldn't avoid suspecting that revenge was an even more powerful motive for the proposition he had just offered her. He knew it would humiliate her to accept his terms, it had humiliated her merely to have them suggested to her, and Daniel wanted to make her pay for the humiliation she had once inflicted on him.

She had often wondered if it hadn't been his ego which had pushed him into asking her to marry him in the first place. A man with Daniel's fierce desire for success would find it hard to take rejection in any shape or form, but particularly where a woman was concerned. The more she got to know him, the more she had realised how that drive to succeed dominated him. Opposition always flicked his ego raw. He was too clever to show it on the surface, he had learnt how to use his charm to get what he wanted, but during their marriage Lindsay had spent a lot of time watching him and she recognised the flicker of anger, the glimmer of hard impatience in his eyes, and she had soon noticed that he would go to any lengths to achieve his ends, use any means; force, charm, money, and especially his own sex appeal. Daniel knew he was attractive to women, damn him, she thought, running an angry hand through her hair.

But if he thought for a minute that he could browbeat her by using her brother's situation to blackmail her, he was going to find out how wrong he was!

I must talk to Stephen, she thought, going to the phone, then stopped, her hand on the receiver. Not yet, Stephen was in no state for that sort of conversation today. She would have to leave a frank discussion until he was more himself.

She forced herself, instead, to do housework and shopping. It helped to turn her mind to more mundane things, the boredom of cleaning the flat and galloping around the supermarket with her trolley was an antidote to the hectic emotional impact of her clash with Daniel. She refused to think about him, she stared at baked beans and washing powder instead with a pretence of interest. The rain had stopped, the sky was a clear, washed blue from which the clouds slowly drifted during the late afternoon. By the time Aston rang her doorbell that evening, the weather was back to high summer.

He looked at her cool, summery dress with a smile. 'You look delicious, what colour do you call that? Asparagus?'

'Lime green, thank you,' Lindsay told him, but laughed. 'Will I need a jacket? What's it like out in the streets?'

'Warm—you're fine as you are,' he assured her. 'I've booked a table at that brasserie where all the film stars go when they're in London, I thought you might enjoy spotting celebrities.'

'How extravagant of you.' Lindsay said, closing the front door. 'It sounds marvellous, thank you.' They walked down, talking about the change in the weather.

His hand touched her bare arm lightly. 'Did you have to use Judo on Daniel Randall, or did he go quietly?'

'Don't let's talk about him.' Lindsay was trying to forget Daniel existed, she did not want to give

Aston a blow-by-blow account of what Daniel had said to her.

'That's fine by me,' said Aston with a wry glance. He was wearing a tailored linen suit, cream and very elegant, under which she saw a dark brown shirt. He looked pretty good himself. 'Don't we make a handsome pair?' Lindsay asked, her green eyes teasing, and he grinned at her. Aston had a strong sense of humour.

As they drove to the restaurant, she asked him: 'What exactly did Stephen tell you on the phone? How serious is his financial problem?'

Aston sobered, staring at the road, his brows meeting. The gold-brown hair gleamed in the last rays of the sun, she saw the tips of his eyelashes glowing gilt too, as he lowered his eyes. His face was not striking, it had too much rugged strength for that, but it pleased her to look at him, his personality came though every time he smiled.

'Bad, I'm afraid,' he said tersely.

'Daniel said something about Stephen being bankrupt. Is it that bad?' Lindsay was nervous as she asked that, she hoped Aston would deny it, but he sighed and shot her a quick look.

'You'll have to ask Stephen that yourself.'

'Does that mean he is, but you'd rather not admit it?'

'It means that Stephen spoke to me in confidence and I can't repeat the details of what he told me.' Aston spoke gently but in a firm tone. 'I know you're very concerned, but the firm is Stephen's business, you really must talk to him, Lindsay.'

She was quiet for a moment, then she said

uncertainly, 'Did he ask you for help, Aston?'
She saw his frown and added hurriedly: 'Please
don't think I'm pressuring you—I have a reason
for asking, believe me.' If Stephen had been
desperate enough to ask Aston for help, Daniel
might be telling the truth.

Aston sighed. 'Purely as a hypothetical case,
Lindsay, even if Stephen had asked me for help I
wouldn't be in any position to give him the sort
of help he would need if he was in danger of
going bankrupt.' He spoke very slowly and
carefully, choosing his words. 'My capital is all
tied up in my shops, I don't have any spare
money floating around.'

'I understand,' Lindsay said flatly.

'Randall would be a much better prospect,'
said Aston, pulling up near the Mayfair brasserie
at which they had booked a table. He turned to
look at her, an arm draped over the wheel. 'He
has the money, but Stephen would have to watch
out for the strings attached to it.'

'Yes,' Lindsay agreed with bitterness.

Aston stared at her. 'And so would you,
Lindsay. He struck me as a very possessive guy,
he didn't like me at all, did he? For an ex-
husband he shows far too much interest in you.'

He had said something like that to her already,
she could see her protests hadn't convinced him
that she was indifferent to Daniel. Pushing a
curling lock of her vivid hair from her flushed
face, she said defiantly: 'Daniel Randall sees
women as objects, and if they've belonged to him,
they're his property even if he rarely sees them.
His vanity wouldn't let him see them any other

way. If he came on like a possessive husband in front of you, that was to make sure you know I'd been his . . .'

'And still were?' Aston murmured, watching her.

'No way.' Lindsay met his eyes levelly. 'He's part of my past, nothing more. I've locked him away with the old photos and theatre programmes.'

'He seems to have escaped,' Aston commented drily, and she laughed, relaxing.

'Houdini is his middle name.'

'So long as you can laugh at him,' he shrugged. 'If you took him seriously, he'd be quite alarming, I should think.'

'Understatement is your forte,' Lindsay agreed. 'Oh, don't talk about him, let's enjoy ourselves and forget Daniel exists.'

'I'll drink to that,' said Aston, getting out of the car, his rugged face alight with dry amusement.

They walked into the restaurant together, talking, and the head waiter came over to greet them politely but without warmth. The place was crowded, every table seemed to be taken, but when Aston mentioned his name the man inclined his head. 'Your table is ready, Mr Hill. Would you like to have a drink at the bar first or . . .'

Aston glanced at her. 'Want a drink, or shall we go to the table right away?'

'We'll go straight in,' said Lindsay, and they followed the head waiter through the closely set tables a moment later. A group was playing on a tiny dais at one end of the room, their blend of traditional jazz kept low so that it didn't interfere with the conversations of clients. As she walked past tables, Lindsay saw any number of familiar faces, the restaurant was a popular night spot with film and stage people.

The head waiter seated her and Aston at a small table in a corner of the room. A blue glass vase holding a white carnation and a spray of feathery fern occupied the centre of the table, and Lindsay glanced up to smile at Aston. 'Pretty, isn't it?' she said, and as her eyes moved away from his amused face she found herself looking at Daniel. He was sitting at a table on the far side of the room and he was watching her with an impassive face. Lindsay felt her face freeze, she looked away quickly, but not before she had noticed the girl sitting opposite him. She was tiny and blonde and very pretty, she was also a familiar face from television since she was one of the stars in a current soap opera. Lindsay both recognised her and was surprised, she looked much smaller and more human in that atmosphere. In that one quick glance, Lindsay took in the stunning red silk dress she wore, the carefully casual chic of her hair-style and the fascinated glow with which she was talking to Daniel. She felt her heart constrict as she looked away.

'Aperitif, madame?' the head waiter was asking.

She forced herself to concentrate. 'Oh, yes, thank you, I'll have a glass of white wine—Sauternes, I think.' She accepted the large menu he handed her and he bent forward to recommend several of the dishes which were the speciality of the house. Lindsay tried to listen, smiling too tightly. She couldn't keep her mind on food while Daniel sat there, one brown hand lying casually on the white tablecloth only an inch away from the blonde girl's fingers. She could see the two hands out of the corner of her eye, she didn't want to watch them but she couldn't help herself.

What was Daniel doing there with that girl? Lindsay couldn't even remember her name, she only knew her face, like everybody else she had watched the soap opera now and then. The girl was too pretty for their relationship to be anything to do with business.

Of course, a girl like that would be a feather in his cap; everyone would recognise her and envy him. Lindsay had never liked the soap opera much, herself, the character the girl played was testy, and silly into the bargain, and from the way she was turning on charm for Daniel she didn't need to do much acting, either. Risking another quick look, Lindsay was rewarded by seeing Daniel's hand touching the other girl's now. Her teeth set and she looked back at the menu fixedly.

'Seen something you like?' Aston asked, and she looked up at him, her eyes wide and startled.

'What?' He had his back to Daniel, she didn't think he had noticed him.

'On the menu,' said Aston, laughing. 'What did you think I meant? I hope you haven't been smitten by some famous star at another table, I wouldn't want to be forced into drastic action to get rid of him.' He put out a hand and took hers, raised it to his lips and kissed it softly. 'I can be possessive, too.'

She smiled at him and felt Daniel's eyes on them, but refused to look in his direction again, angry with herself for the brief, agonising stab of jealousy she had felt as she saw him touch the other girl's hand. She wouldn't let herself care, hadn't she learnt even now that Daniel Randall refused to belong to anybody? Tonight he was here with a blonde, tomorrow he would be with someone else. It was none of her business, thank heavens, he could date a whole harem and she wouldn't care!

'I'm having difficulty choosing, it all reads like a poem.'

'The chef is a very good,' Aston agreed. 'That's why it's so popular.'

'Crowded, isn't it?' Lindsay let her eyes move around the room, being careful not to look towards Daniel's table. 'I can see why it takes all evening to be served.'

She let her gaze drift casually over Daniel and felt her throat close up in agitation at the expression in those hard, grey eyes. He looked grim, his jaw taut, his mouth straight, and Lindsay was angrily pleased, she felt a fierce rush of satisfaction at knowing that Daniel was not pleased to see her with Aston. It might only be a dog-in-the-manger sense of possession because she had been his wife, but at least he wasn't indifferent, and despite the melting smiles of his blonde companion his attention was on what was happening at Lindsay's table rather than his own. Lindsay liked that, she smiled at Aston over her menu.

'I think I'll start with the Waldorf salad,' she said. 'I like this place, it's fun.'

'Good,' said Aston, his eyes wrinkling in amusement. 'I told you we would enjoy ourselves, didn't I?'

'So you did,' Lindsay agreed. 'And that's just what I mean to do . . .' And then she had a twinge of conscience about him, because she knew she was far more interested in scoring off Daniel than she was in Aston. Keeping her eyes firmly on Aston's face, she asked: 'How are your sister's twins? They must be nearly two by now, or is it three?'

'Three,' he said, smiling, and settled down to talk about his family while she listened intently, and did not allow herself to look away. Why couldn't she fall in love with Aston? He was a fantastic man, the nicest she knew, he was funny and kind and attractive, and she ought to be mad about him, anyone with any sense would adore him. An intelligent girl wouldn't even be aware there was any other man in the room; certainly not one who was selfish, egotistic, totally ruthless and hadn't a scruple to his name.

CHAPTER SIX

DANIEL rang her the following evening. She had spent the day with Aston, in the country, and had barely got back into her flat when the phone rang. The weather had been gorgeous all day, Lindsay had sunbathed in a tiny white bikini, and her skin had that tight, warm glow the sun leaves, she felt lazy and relaxed, she was still smiling after Aston's parting remark. Aston always made her smile, and today he had helped her to banish Daniel from her mind, but as she picked up the phone Daniel sprang back again like the Demon King in a pantomime, scattering her thoughts.

'Where the hell have you been all day?' he demanded without telling her who it was—not that he needed to, Lindsay knew at once from the first syllable. 'I've been ringing since early this morning—did you spend the night with him?'

'Hallo, Daniel,' she said while she tried to gather herself together, then could have kicked herself. It would have been much better to say: 'Who *is* that?'

'Did you?' Daniel repeated, his voice harsh.

'Did I what?' she fenced.

'You haven't been at home all day, where have you been? I told you I was going to ring you.'

'I spent the day visiting Aston's sister, she lives in the country. It's a long drive, Aston picked me up at eight o'clock this morning.'

'Visiting his sister? How cosy—his intentions must be serious.' Daniel's voice held a sneer.

'You sound like a Victorian father.' Two could play at that game, if Daniel wanted to turn nasty Lindsay was more than happy to do the same.

'Can he lend Stephen enough to keep the factory going?' Daniel put a bite into that question and Lindsay winced. She didn't answer and after a brief silence, Daniel asked: 'Well, have you thought over my offer?'

'I've tried not to think about it at all,' she muttered, and he laughed shortly.

'I'm sure you have.'

'It's too disgusting!' Lindsay spat that at him, her hand gripping the phone so tightly that her knuckles turned white.

'Take it or leave it,' Daniel shrugged. 'Stephen's your brother, he isn't mine, nobody does anything without getting something back.' He sounded brisk and businesslike and she hated him, then his voice deepened and darkened. 'And Aston Hill's out of the picture, for a start,' he added. 'I don't want him around in future.'

Lindsay thought of the blonde actress he had been with last night and her skin burned with fury. 'You're not dictating my life to me—I had enough of that when we were married!'

'Up to you,' Daniel said tersely. 'If Stephen hasn't paid back that bank loan by next Friday he'll have to liquidate. You have until Thursday to decide.' He slammed the phone down and she jerked as her eardrum rang with the noise. She put back her own receiver, her hand fumbling, trembling, then looked at her watch. It was gone nine, too late to ring Stephen. She would have to talk to him tomorrow, he should have recovered a little by then.

When she got to her office next day she found her boss lying back in his chair with his feet on the table and his eyes closed, his face turned towards the sunshine streaming in at the window. Chris was a calm, lazy man who moved very rarely and when he did performed each action with the considered grace of a two-toed sloth. Small, slightly built, with smooth blond hair and bright blue eyes, he would have been exceptionally good-looking if it had not been for that lack of vitality. His face was happy but distinctly unimpressive.

'Busy as usual, I see,' Lindsay remarked, standing in the doorway of his office and watching him with resigned amusement.

Chris opened one eye to observe her. He flapped a welcoming hand, 'Hi.' The effort of speech apparently exhausted him, his eye closed and he sank back into golden slumber.

'Have those stills come yet?' Lindsay asked, cruelly insisting that he should make some pretence of working.

The hand flapped at his desk. She saw a large brown envelope lying on it and went over to pick it up, shooting a small pile of glossy photographs on to the desk. She leaned over, a hand propping her up, and spread them out, recognising some faces, looking at others with curiosity. Most of the girls in the photographs were models, some were actresses, and over the month Lindsay and

Chris had seen hundreds of different girls without feeling that any one of them was the girl they were looking for, the girl whose face would fit an image they wanted.

Vivons were about to launch a new range of cosmetics and they wanted someone very special to appear in their advertising campaign. The managing director of the firm had begun to be impatient, because so far they hadn't come up with what he called 'The Face.'

'It's hopeless, Charles won't go for any of these,' Lindsay said gloomily. 'They don't say a thing to *me*—what about you?'

Chris turned a thumb downwards without opening his eyes. He didn't waste time or energy in pointless discussion, yet he always managed to get what he wanted, although Lindsay often wondered how he did it. Whatever magic he performed, he did it when nobody was looking. Every time you saw him he seemed to be asleep, but Vivons would have fought tooth and nail to keep him if another firm tried to steal him away.

'Perhaps we're going about this the wrong way,' said Lindsay, sitting down on the edge of the desk and swinging her legs. 'We're waiting for The Face to come and find us, maybe we should go out and find her.'

Chris opened both eyes, they looked at her, so blue they sparkled like clear sapphires, and she stared into them, raising her brows.

'What do you think?'

'Keep talking,' Chris encouraged, shifting very slightly in his chair and crossing his feet. He almost always wore jeans and a thin, tightly fitting shirt open at the neck and worn without a tie. Shoes were his one extravagance, he had them hand-made for him because his feet were incredibly small and thin for a man and he could never get mass-produced shoes that fitted. Today he was wearing soft, supple blue leather, so velvety it made you want to stroke it.

'Why don't we draw up a list of what we're looking for? Should she be brunette or . . .'

'Blonde,' Chris decided. 'With the sexy, sweet look of a Marilyn Monroe, we don't want to put women off buying the range, they've got to like her, want to look like her.' For him that was an enormously long statement. He had obviously been thinking about it, he knew precisely what he was looking for, Lindsay should have known he wasn't just haphazard in his search.

'Why do you let me talk myself into looking silly?' she asked wryly. 'You had it all worked out already, didn't you? Why didn't you tell all the agencies you were looking for a sexy blonde? Then they wouldn't keep showering us with girls we can't use?'

'One of them might be perfect,' he said, his wide mouth amused. 'A brunette we can always dye into a blonde, it's the face that matters, not the hair colour,' he yawned, running a hand through his hair. 'I'll know her when I see her.'

The phone rang and Lindsay picked it up, listened, then handed it to Chris. 'Charles,' she mouthed.

He cradled the phone on his thin shoulder. 'Hi, Charles,' he murmured. Lindsay shuffled through the photographs again, her eyes almost blurring with boredom. The girls were all so beautiful, so perfectly packaged, so plastic—when you had seen one you had seen them all, she found it hard to distinguish one from another. Vivons did not a want a girl people couldn't remember, they wanted someone whose face made people rush out to buy their cosmetics.

'Not yet,' said Chris. 'But we'll find her, don't worry.'

Lindsay slid off the desk and went over to the window to stare down at the street below. London hummed and roared all around them, the roads thick with traffic, the buildings throbbing with noise and people. Somewhere out there was the girl they were looking for, but how could they find her when the agencies kept coming up with the same girls everybody used? They wanted someone new, someone with immediate impact, someone so special she focused the eye and held it.

'Don't flap,' Chris said lazily. 'Charles, just leave it with me—I'll come up with the right girl in time.'

A moment later he put the phone down and Lindsay turned to look at him wryly. He smiled and closed his eyes.

London was sweltering in heat all day, Lindsay found it hard to concentrate, her thin yellow cotton dress was sticking to her and every time she moved she felt perspiration trickle down her spine. Chris was in apparent hibernation, whenever she went into his office she found him in the same position, eyes shut, body limp. For once she felt like following suit, it was much too hot to work, but somebody had to keep the routine jobs going and from the start Chris had made it plain that that was what she was there for; he needed a girl who could carry his workload as well as her own. At times she had resented doing two people's work, but now she realised that in his way Chris was a genius; his methods were his own, but they succeeded, which, in that business, was all that counted, so Lindsay worked on without complaining.

By the time she left the office that evening she was exhausted, her spirits as flat as a pancake. She took the tube to Stephen's nearest station, feeling sticky and grubby and dying for a long, cold shower. First, though, she must talk to Stephen.

Alice opened the door to her. She was wearing jeans, a T-shirt and a printed plastic apron, and her face was flushed.

'Oh, it's you,' she said, moving back to let Lindsay walk past.

'Hot, isn't it?' Lindsay could hear the children playing in the garden, their voices cheerful. She walked into the kitchen. Alice had been chopping cucumber, the smell of it filled the air. 'How's Stephen?' Lindsay asked, lowering her voice as Alice joined her and closed the door.

'He's in the garage working on his car,' said Alice.

'Is he okay?' Lindsay wasn't sure how to talk to Alice, her sister-in-law seemed rather aggressive today, it wasn't like her.

'I wouldn't know,' said Alice, picking up her small kitchen knife and chopping with noisy conviction.

'Oh,' Lindsay said, watching her in dismay. People were acting out of character all round her, she didn't know this Alice whose face had set like concrete and who was slicing the cucumber as though she was guillotining an enemy.

'I'm not talking to him,' Alice told her, chop, chop. 'If you want to know how he is, better ask him.' Chop, chop. 'He doesn't confide in me, I'm only his wife.' Having despatched the cucumber she looked around for something else to use her knife on; so Lindsay decided to leave and talk to Stephen. It seemed wiser.

He was inside his car bonnet, only his legs visible. 'Hallo,' Lindsay said to them, and Stephen turned his head to peer.

'Oh, hello, Lindsay, when did you get here? Have you been into the house?'

'Alice is getting the supper,' Lindsay told him. 'I think.' Either that or the cucumber-chopping was therapy, she thought. Stephen extricated himself from the bonnet, wiping his hands on a filthy piece of rag. She watched him, trying to read his expression, which wasn't difficult, he looked drained and pale and quite hopeless.

'I wanted to talk to you,' she told him, and he nodded.

'I'm sorry Alice dragged you into all this . . .'

'Don't be silly, you're my brother, of course I'm concerned. I'm glad she did ring me.'

'I should have rung her earlier, don't think I don't know that, I just couldn't think of anything to say to her.' Stephen kept on wiping his hands as though trying to erase more than the stain of black oil, and Lindsay felt like crying. He looked so defeated.

'How bad is it?' she asked tentatively, and he grimaced, his eyes down.

'I'm wiped out.' He flung the rag into the back seat of the car and closed the bonnet, still without looking at her.

'Have you tried . . .' she began, and Stephen turned those weary eyes on her, their rims pink as though he had been crying. Her stomach turned over and she bit the inside of her lip.

'I've tried everything I can think of,' he said. 'Short of a miracle, I've had it—know any good miracle-workers?'

'Daniel,' she began, and Stephen laughed curtly.

'Has too much hard-headed business sense to be bothered with me. Do you think that didn't occur to me? No, I'll have to declare myself bankrupt, sell up everything and get a job.' He paused, his body wrenched by a deep sigh. 'If I can, if anyone will employ me—I know I wouldn't.' He walked round the car and Lindsay followed slowly. She had never expected to feel so deeply worried about Stephen, he had always been the one who worried about her; now their positions had been reversed and it made her feel uncertain of herself, she wasn't sure how to handle the situation, how to talk to him.

'Don't do anything in a hurry,' she said to his back. 'Wait for a few days . . .'

'Don't tell me something may turn up,' Stephen muttered. 'I can do without the bromides.' He opened the front door. From the kitchen they heard Alice talking to the children in a brisk, no-nonsense voice. Stephen sighed again. 'She's furious with me, and I can't blame her. I should have told her, but I just couldn't face it. I didn't have the guts.'

'She'll forgive you,' Lindsay assured him, hoping she was right.

'We'll have to leave this house, it will have to go,' he said. 'Alice will hate that, she loves this place.'

The kitchen door opened and he stopped talking. Alice ignored him, looking at Lindsay. 'Are you staying for supper?' It was very far from being an invitation and Lindsay hurriedly pretended to smile.

'I'd have loved to,' she lied. 'But I've got a date, I just called in to see how Stephen was.' Alice's face was stony; that remark didn't go down at all well. 'I must rush,' Lindsay added quickly, gave her brother a quick kiss on the cheek and fled. She felt resentful as she made her way back to her own flat. Alice was being very unsympathetic, why was she punishing Stephen when it must be so obvious that he was miserable? Lindsay had been angry with her brother herself, while he was missing, she had understood then why Alice was so angry, but face to face with Stephen's helpless defeat, how could Alice go on being unkind to him?

When she got home, she stripped and had a cool shower, washing away the city dust and stale perspiration of the day, her thirsty skin drinking in the water through every pore. She towelled her hair lightly, slipped into a short white towelling robe and padded into the kitchen. It was far too hot to eat, she decided, looking into the fridge. She got herself a long, cool drink and went into the sitting-room, flinging herself down on the couch with a sigh.

What was she going to do? If she had ever had any hope that Daniel was lying it had evaporated in the face of Stephen's despair. She couldn't let her brother's firm and home be taken away from him if she could stop it, she owed Stephen too much; he had carried the burden of managing their home for years, he hadn't married until Lindsay herself had married, all his life he had been strong, responsible, hard-working. Now he needed her help—how could she refuse it?

As she sipped her drink the phone rang and she started nervously, almost swallowing a piece of ice. Putting down the glass, she went over to pick up the phone.

'Hallo?' Her voice sounded low and wary, she was afraid it would be Daniel, and she was only too right.

'Thought about it yet?'

A flare of rage went through her. 'I thought you gave me until Thursday to make up my mind?'

'Just making sure you don't forget about it,' he said mockingly.

'As if I was likely to!'

'You have a genius for forgetting things,' he said, and the words carried a heavy load of sarcasm. There was a pause, then he asked drily: 'No date tonight? Or is Hill there?'

'No, he isn't,' Lindsay snapped, then wished she had lied—Aston made a good cover, but she hated herself for using him as one. Quickly she said: 'But he may come round later.' It was true enough, Aston had said he might call in at the flat some time that evening. He was having dinner with one of his suppliers, if the evening ended early Aston would try to get to see her, but if the other man felt like talking for hours over drinks, Aston wouldn't make it.

'You looked very pretty last night,' Daniel said softly, and she felt a shudder run down her spine. 'That dress suits you, green is your colour, it makes your eyes look brighter.' His voice seemed to stroke her skin, she despised herself for trembling.

'I'm surprised you noticed—you seemed too busy looking into your girl-friend's eyes. How did you pick her up? Don't tell me you've started manufacturing soap?'

'Miaow,' he mocked, laughing, and she was furious with herself for coming on like a jealous woman.

'I met her to talk business,' Daniel said, and Lindsay laughed angrily.

'You don't expect me to believe that? Nobody talks business with a blonde sex kitten over a lengthy dinner.'

'Carolyn used to model for us before she went into acting,' he told her. 'We're trying to persuade her to do some more work.'

'What sort?' Lindsay asked sarcastically. 'And where? The bedroom, by any chance? Auditioning her last night, were you?'

'Careful,' he drawled. 'Your claws are showing, pussycat.'

Lindsay flung the phone down and walked away. The angry exchange had been bitterly familiar, how many times had she heard herself sniping at him like that over some other girl? She had never seemed able to stop herself, the jealousy had sprung up inside her and she had been shaking with it, she had wanted to scream, hit him, slap the other girl. When they were alone the black emotion had come pouring out of her, and only afterwards when she had calmed down had she been able to think clearly. Then she had felt sick, ashamed, shabby, and she had hated herself.

She wrapped her arms around her body, bent over, fighting the stabbing knives of misery that were tearing at her. Her jealousy had ruined her marriage, she had been so uncertain of herself, of Daniel, she hadn't been able to believe he could really love her and she had despised herself. The intensity of her feelings for him left her scared, she was terrified that someone else would take him away from her. She was so ordinary, so young and unsophisticated, how could she hope to hold a man like him? Every time he looked at anyone else, every time another woman looked at him, fear had tormented her. She had told herself that Daniel had only married her because she wouldn't sleep with him, and she had waited for him to wander away to fresh woods and pastures new. She knew the sort of life he had led before they married, he was far too attractive to be content with one woman, she knew he must be bored with her.

It had been so easy to convince herself, their marriage hadn't a hope of success from the start. When she left him, she hated him for the pain she had suffered for months, the pain which refused to die down even after their divorce, but over the past year she had managed to evict him from her mind. It hadn't been easy, some nights she had wallowed in grief only to get up next day and despise herself for giving way to an outworn emotion. Aston had helped, dating him had given her other things to think about. Why had fate brought Daniel Randall back into her life?

She finished her drink and watched a programme on TV to take her mind off Daniel. Aston didn't show up, presumably his supplier had had other plans. At ten o'clock, Lindsay went to bed and lay in the darkness giving herself a stern lecture. She was not going to get involved with Daniel Randall again. He was bad for her, it made her ill to feel jealous, and if she let herself think about him she would start being jealous of every girl he saw. She couldn't reach the source of her jealousy with her reason, it didn't respond to logic; it was bitter, obsessive, destructive, and she refused to let it take her over again.

Chris didn't arrive at the office next morning until after eleven. He wandered in, sleek and lithe in his usual jeans and shirt, moving at his normal pace and Lindsay glanced up from a desk covered with paper. 'Good heavens, don't say you've decided to do some work?'

He sleepily propped himself against her door. 'Anything happen?'

'The sky fell in, that's all.'

He surveyed her through lowered lids, unexcited. 'Any casualties?'

'Charles rang. He sounded like a man in a state of panic. He wanted to know when you meant to get off your chair and do something to find The Face.'

'Did he ask where I was?'

'What do you think?' Lindsay leaned back in her chair and smiled at him. 'I told him you were out hunting for the girl of his dreams.'

Chris put two fingers to his lips and blew her a kiss, and she laughed, shaking her head at him.

'He also asked if you'd have lunch with him,' she pointed out. 'So that he could harangue you on the subject for a few hours.'

'What did you tell him?'

'That I thought you had an appointment.'

'So I do,' said Chris, ruffling his blond hair thoughtfully as he stared at her. 'And so do you, my angel.'

'Do I?' She leaned over to flick open her desk diary. 'I haven't written it down—who with?'

'Me,' he said. 'We're going to have a long, quiet lunch and put our thinking caps on . . .'

'I thought you had yours on already,' she said, glancing down at the pile of work she had in front of her. 'Chris, I've got to get all this stuff done.' She had been working flat out since nine o'clock that morning, but she didn't seem to have made any dent in the work which had been piling up in her in-tray for days. None of it was urgent, which was why she had left it untouched for so long, but it had to be done sooner or later, and she was in the right mood to be efficient.

'It can wait,' Chris said as he strolled away. Lindsay glared after him—that was the motto he lived by, everything could wait and usually did. What was amazing was that he got away with it. Problems he left unsolved seemed to solve themselves, letters that didn't get written ceased to be necessary, people he ignored went away without complaining. He was just born lucky, she decided.

'Lady on the phone, came out in a rash after using Moonglow Seventy-Nine,' her secretary said on the intercom, and, sighing, Lindsay picked up the phone, her voice automatically becoming soothing, horrified, sympathetic.

She had no sooner put down the phone again than her door opened and one of Vivons sales team came in to complain about the way complaints were handled by the office. 'I'm sick of promising we'd look into it,' he said, perching on her desk and picking up her pen. She watched him doodling with it on a spare piece of paper as he talked.

'I'll give the complaints section a talking-to,' she promised.

'Don't forget,' he said, sliding off the desk. He looked at her with appreciation and gave a coaxing grin. 'Have lunch with me and we'll discuss it further.'

'Sorry, I have a date.' Lindsay put out her hand. 'Thank you.'

He was putting her pen into his jacket pocket. Blankly, he said: 'What?'

'Pen,' she said.

'Oh, sorry, just habit,' he said, handing the pen

back with his eyes on the smooth curve of her figure from her high, rounded breasts to her slim hips. He backed out, talking and staring. Lindsay made a face at the door after it had shut behind him. He had a fantastic sales record, buyers ate out of his hand, and she could see why: he responded to women like a man in a desert spotting an oasis, and most buyers working with cosmetics were women, it was not a male territory. Lindsay found it irritating to try to work with a man who couldn't stop looking at her figure. Given half a chance, he would use his hands as well as his eyes, he was a bottom pincher and an arm fondler. Her secretary came in, flushed, and wailed: 'I'm black and blue! I should get danger money!'

'Sorry, Ann,' said Lindsay, laughing. 'Next time he comes in, keep the desk between you,' and Ann said she would remember that.

Lindsay dictated several letters, read a few of the snarling memos which their managing director was fond of despatching around the building, then tried to get back to her paperwork, only to have Chris saunter in and ask: 'Coming?'

'It isn't lunchtime already!' she protested, looking at her watch. It was almost one o'clock. 'Where's the morning gone?' Lindsay moaned, pushing back her chair and getting up. 'I haven't done anything!'

'You should be organised,' Chris told her. 'Like me.' He yawned, his thumbs in his jeans back pockets, and she eyed him with suppressed fury. A lot of the paperwork she was wading through should have gone to him, but if it had, he would have dealt with it by the simple method of screwing it up and chucking it into the nearest wastepaper basket.

'I'm going to the cloakroom,' she announced with dignity, and walked out. The office was almost empty, everyone else had gone to lunch, only the office junior remained at her desk, eating an apple and drinking a low-calorie orange juice.

As Chris and Lindsay left five minutes later, the girl smiled at them, gazing at Chris with wide-eyed eagerness. Everyone in the office liked him, he had a smile for everyone, but then they didn't have to do his work for him, they didn't have to run around in his wake dealing with all the problems Chris decided to ignore.

He took her to lunch at a small back-street restaurant that took its time over serving you and didn't seem to mind how long you took to eat your meal. The menu was limited and Italian, groaning with calories. Lindsay skipped past the tempting pasta and ordered melon, then chose a main course of chicken with a side salad. Chris ate his way through a banquet, rich in sauces and highly spiced, but then he always did eat without caring about calories and got away with it. He was as thin as a rake, it wasn't fair.

Sighing, Lindsay slowly ate her melon while Chris twirled spaghetti on his fork. 'This is delicious, you should have had some,' he told her.

She averted her eyes. 'Are we really going to discuss The Face? Have you had any new ideas?'

'I'm hoping some will come,' he said, his eye roving over the other tables. 'What we want is a new face . . .'

'Someone who isn't a professional model, you mean?' Lindsay asked, and he looked back her, blue eyes blazing.

'Why not?' he stopped talking, stared at her fixedly. 'Like you,' he said. 'You're the sort of girl I'm looking for—a girl with a vital, alive face, someone special but not artificial.'

Lindsay laughed, her green eyes vivid with amusement. 'You'll never sell that idea to Charles, he'll send you to the funny farm.'

Chris put down his fork, his face alight. 'I'm serious, I just looked at you properly and you're terrific. Bone structure sensational, eyes beautifully spaced, good nose . . .'

'Hey, do you mind?' She was beginning to get alarmed, she did not like being analysed feature by feature, even though Chris was being heavily flattering. She knew he was using only the best butter, he didn't mean those things, and it made her feel uncomfortable.

'Sexy mouth,' he said, taking no notice. 'Nice rounded chin, slim neck.'

'Stop it!' she protested, very flushed, then, as his eyes moved lower and he opened his mouth, 'I mean it—you can stop right there.' She did not want to hear his description of her breasts, the way he was looking at her made her feel like a slave on the auction block, she objected to his stare and his personal comments.

'What's the matter?' he asked, all innocence. The blue eyes were open and frank, smiling at her. 'I'm perfectly serious.'

'Don't be so ridiculous,' Lindsay muttered.

'It came to me in a flash,' said Chris, looking

quite excited for him. 'I looked at you and I knew
. . . you're The Face.'

CHAPTER SEVEN

'I DON'T think that's funny,' Lindsay said.

Chris leaned towards her, his fingertips drumming on the table. 'But don't you see—it could be you? It could be her.' he flung out a hand at the small, dark waitress who was serving the next table. 'It could be that tall blonde over there. It could be anyone.'

She relaxed. 'Well, obviously . . .'

'Hang on,' he said impatiently. 'I haven't finished my point. We're not looking for a professional model, we're looking for an ordinary girl. So where do we look?'

Lindsay thought, frowning. 'Well, I suppose . . .' She hadn't got a clue.

'We run a competition,' Chris said triumphantly.

Her mouth parted on a gasp, and he laughed at her expression, nodding.

'That's right, a competition,' he repeated. 'For our girl, The Face, the girl who could be anyone in the country.' He was talking faster than she had ever heard him talk before, his words tumbling over each other to get out. 'Anyone who wants to enter will have to buy one of our products to get an entry form. They have to send in their photograph and . . .'

'My word!' Lindsay had caught fire from him, she was so staggered she couldn't think of anything else to say, so she said: 'My word !' again, and he laughed, highly delighted.

'Think Charles will like it?'

'He'll eat it,' she said without a shred of doubt. 'It will be terrific publicity, it will sell products like hot cakes and we'll get an entirely new face out of it, someone special is bound to be thrown up by a campaign like that.' She looked at him with admiration. 'You're a genius!'

Chris relapsed into his normal torpor, smiling lazily. 'You've noticed at last! I wondered how long it would take for the light to dawn.'

'Did it just come to you in a flash?' Lindsay asked curiously. 'I mean . . . just now? Did you really just think it up or . . .'

'I've had it hovering around my mind,' he admitted. 'Ideas are like that sometimes, you just catch a glimpse of them out of the corner of your mind's eye, then they're gone, but if you sit round without worrying and wait—they come back.'

'So that's what you're doing for most of the day,' she said drily. 'Just waiting for ideas. I've often wondered.'

'Nasty,' he said, grinning.

'Finish your spaghetti,' she advised. 'You've deserved it. You ought to eat fish, really, for brain power.'

'Spaghetti works even better,' Chris assured her, turning his attention to his plate.

They walked back to the office in brilliant sunshine, waves of heat coming up from the pavements, the cars driving past giving off metallic flashes of reflected light. Charles was

going to be over the moon, thought Lindsay.
Chris had come up with his best idea ever.

All that afternoon she was caught up in the
maelstrom which Chris's brainwave had caused.
She didn't have a chance to do any of the routine
work, she was too busy discussing the details of
the campaign with Charles and the other top
executives of the company. Chris always left such
minor matters to other people. Having done his
part, he collapsed in a chair like a rag doll and
smiled beatifically on them, saying almost
nothing. Nobody minded, he could do no wrong
today.

While she talked and listened, Lindsay's
mind kept wandering away to the subject that
was engrossing her secret attention, but she
refused to let herself dwell on Daniel's proposition. He had given her until Thursday to make
a decision, and it was already Tuesday, which
left her only two days. Every time she faced
that fact, she felt an icy dart of anxiety. He had
left her without options, she couldn't think of
any way of saving Stephen from bankruptcy.
Glancing at Chris, she wished she had his
inspiration—she could do with a brainwave
herself.

If Daniel had walked out on her, he wouldn't
want to hurt and humiliate her now, but she had
committed the unforgivable sin by walking out on
him. He might have lost interest in her, he might
have regretted getting married at all, but his ego
couldn't take the shock of having her end their
marriage. That had been Daniel's privilege, his
choice—he had decided to marry her in the first

place and he felt aggrieved because she had had the temerity to leave him.

Lindsay had no doubts about his motives. He was using her brother as a weapon against her. He must hate her, she thought, staring at the ceiling. It hurt, she felt cold and on the point of tears, but however she felt she still had to make up her mind what to do, and there was no one she could confide in, it would be too painful to tell anyone. This was one decision she had to make alone, without advice.

Aston rang just before she left the office. 'I'm working late tonight, but tomorrow should be an easier day. Could we have dinner?'

'Love to,' Lindsay said warmly. She wished she dared tell him about Daniel's blackmail, but what could he do?

'Miss you,' he said softly and she smiled.

'Same here. Don't work too hard. I'll see you tomorrow.'

'I'll pick you up at the flat at seven,' he said before ringing off. Lindsay put down the phone, sighing. She made her way home in the rush-hour traffic, her clothes sticking to her again, the heatwave showed no sign of diminishing. People were irritable, impatient, flushed, many of them showing signs of sun-worship, their faces and arms reddened. Men were in shirt-sleeves, tie-less. Women were in thin summer dresses, their legs bare. Lindsay wondered if she looked the way they did; her skin beaded with perspiration, her eyes tired, her movements lethargic. That was how she felt, she had no energy at all, she just wanted to flop out and keep still. This was no weather to be in a city, she longed to be on a beach.

When she got back to the flat she showered and put on a brief white cotton tunic cut on simple lines; the neck low and rounded, the hem just above her knees and the sides split for easy movement. It had a Grecian look, she had bought it in Athens on a holiday a year ago but had rarely worn it because the cotton was so thin it was more like gauze and totally transparent. It was not a dress she could wear to the office or in the streets, but it was perfect for relaxing in weather like this; the filmy material floated around her as she walked, she felt free and at ease.

She had a glass of lime-juice and a tiny salad, then lay on the couch listening to Spanish guitar music.

The doorbell went, and her heart skipped a beat, then hammered inside her ribcage, making her feel sick. She stumbled to the floor, dropping her book. She knew who it was before she got to the front door of the flat and opened it—every instinct shrieked a warning.

He leaned against the door; very tall and powerful, a lean-hipped, unsmiling man with narrowed grey eyes that openly took in every detail of her appearance, travelling from her curling, still damp hair to the quivering curve of her pink lips, down over the curve of her body in the far too revealing, gauzy dress. Lindsay bore that look with nervous defiance, her chin up.

'I'm busy!'

Daniel smiled with dry sarcasm and walked past her with such cool confidence that she made no attempt to stop him. Closing the door slowly, she followed and found him standing in the sitting-room, looking at the book on the floor, the empty glass. Without a word he went over to the record player and lifted the arm. The guitar music stopped mid-beat.

'Do you mind? You've got a nerve!' Lindsay burst out, and he turned to survey her with a crooked little smile.

'I like the dress.' But it wasn't at the dress that he was looking, it was at what was under it, and Lindsay felt her skin burn. Helplessly, she wished she had put on something else, she might as well be naked.

'What's the matter?' Daniel mocked, watching her with eyes which pinned her to the spot.

'What do you want?' she asked shakily, and he laughed.

'Care to re-phrase the question?'

'Aren't you witty?' she muttered, hating him. 'You know what I mean—why are you here?'

'I can't keep away from you,' said Daniel with the same mockery, and her temper flared.

'You've managed it for two years!'

His smile hardened and the grey eyes were fierce with an emotion she couldn't decipher. 'I wasn't coming crawling after you on my knees.'

Her throat tightened. 'What's different now?' she flung back at him, refusing to believe the force she heard in his voice.

'Now it's going to be you on your knees,' he said through his teeth, his eyes harsh, and she went cold from head to foot. 'I only deal on my own terms,' Daniel added. 'You didn't think I'd accept yours? You left me, I wasn't chasing after you, but now you'll come back knowing I own you.'

What he was saying came as no real surprise to her, she knew she had wounded his ego and she knew Daniel's pride was monolithic, his sense of himself impenetrable, unshakable, but hearing him state his hostility so openly made her tremble in shock.

'You can't own human beings,' she stammered, nevertheless, holding her head up and refusing to betray the fear which had swallowed her.

His eyes flashed with bitter humour. 'Can't you? That depends on your definition of ownership. If you want to save your brother's neck, you'll come back to me, and on my terms.'

She was so angry her teeth were chattering. 'You're crazy,' she said. 'You won't get much enjoyment out of forcing me to . . .'

'Won't I?' he asked, moving with a speed that made her jump in alarm.

She didn't have time to escape, the next second he had one arm around her while the other forced up her chin. Rigid and shaking, Lindsay looked into the hard grey eyes, her mouth dry.

'Don't,' she whispered, and Daniel's eyes glittered as he smiled in threat.

'That's one word you'll never use to me again.' His mouth came down on her lips, burning with a fever she felt leaping up inside herself, and it did not matter that his hunger was born out of hatred and a wish to humiliate her, the demand of the kiss was met by an answering demand in her, desire fountained inside her body and she weakened in his arms, swaying towards him. Bending her backwards, Daniel slid his mouth down her throat and with closed eyes she trembled, a husky little moan breathed through her crushed lips. Behind her lids, light flashed and gleamed, she was dizzy and hot.

'You want me,' Daniel muttered, his mouth at the base of her throat, and she sighed, shuddering with pleasure, feeling his hand moving under the gauze, stroking the smooth flesh of her thigh.

Her arms went round his neck, she touched his hair, his nape, the muscled shoulders, her lips parted, aching for the touch of his mouth. Her mind had given up trying to think, she was in a state of weak confusion, the throb of desire in her body dominating her. Daniel's hands explored the naked flesh beneath her dress, caressing her warm breasts while she trembled, feeling the urgency inside him and knowing she felt it, too, a mounting need which grew with every movement of his hands. He was breathing quickly, thickly, she could hear his heart thudding in the same wild rhythm as her own.

She began to be frightened by the intensity of her feelings, a part of her standing aside like a voyeur, whispering mental warnings. She was letting Daniel have things all his own way, she was out of control, her mind had no part in what was happening. He was pulling the thin material down from her shoulders, bending his head to kiss the hardened nipples on her breasts, and that separated part of her protested, despised her for the husky little moans he was wringing out of her.

What had he just said? That she would never say no to him again? That would make her a puppet, without a mind of its own, and wasn't that how she was behaving now, moaning in abandoned excitement while he touched her?

This was not lovemaking, it was a deliberate, cynical manipulation of her body by a man who wanted to humiliate her, and she was playing the accomplice to her own destruction when if she had an ounce of self-respect she would stop him and throw him out of her life again.

She wrenched herself away, her breathing husky and impeded. Daniel stared at her and she stood facing him, trembling, her gauzy dress half off, her bare shoulders and breasts exposed.

'No,' she said, her hands clenched.

His eyes darkened, his jaw taut. 'That wasn't the message I was getting a moment ago. You wanted it . . .'

'No!' she said again, much louder, to drown what he was saying, to drown the feverish admission of her own body.

'What's the matter? Afraid Hill will walk in? Has a key, does he?' Daniel was angry enough now to grind the words out through teeth that barely parted, rage showed in the grey eyes.

'Aston has nothing to do with this!'

'Hasn't he?'

'It's you,' Lindsay said incoherently. 'I won't let you do this to me.'

'You're lying to yourself if you think I'm doing anything you don't want me to do,' he broke out angrily. 'You wanted me to make love to you. Oh, you'd have died rather than admit it to me, you prefer to get me to force you, don't you? Then you can tell yourself you weren't responsible, I made you do it, but that's a lie. I can have you any time I want you.'

'Get out!' she shouted, tension making her body shake.

'You've always had a frigid fear of sex,' he went on, ignoring her.

'I'm not frigid and I'm not afraid of sex, I don't have to be either to refuse to go to bed with you, you know!' Lindsay was insulted by his accusation.

'When we first met, you were practically walled in ice,' Daniel sneered. 'I had to chip my way through. I got frostbite just touching your hand.'

She was white. 'You swine! I was only just out of school . . .'

'What was it? A convent?'

'Just because I wouldn't let you rush me into bed on our first date!'

'I had to make it respectable by putting a ring on your hand first, didn't I?' he snarled, and Lindsay slapped his face so hard his head jerked back in surprise. He looked at her with dangerous eyes for a split second and before she had moved again his own hand came up and to her disbelief she felt it sting her cheek. Shock brought tears to her eyes, Daniel was darkly flushed, his brows black above brooding, angry eyes.

'Don't ever hit me again or next time I'll do more than give you a token slap!' he grated.

She touched the hot mark on her cheek with her fingertips and he watched her, frowning.

'Did that make you feel better?' she asked

contemptuously. 'You get your kicks in a funny way.'

'You hit me first, but then that's typical—you provoke a reaction, then turn round and complain about it. Right from the first, you've done the same thing. When we met you kept giving me inviting smiles, but promise was one thing, delivery something else, wasn't it?'

'You just had a one-track mind. In my book accepting a dinner date doesn't mean you automatically go to bed with a man.'

His smile was hard. 'How long did Hill have to wait?'

'I haven't . . .' She stopped, biting her lip, and Daniel's eyes widened and gleamed.

'Well, well, well,' he said softly, and smiled. 'Haven't you, now? He must be one hell of a patient guy—and very frustrated.'

Lindsay did not like his smile, it held too much satisfaction and far too much self-congratulation. If she hadn't been afraid of his response, she'd have hit him again, but the glowing mark on her cheek urged caution.

'And so must you be,' he added slowly, watching her as a hot tide of colour ran up her face. 'Two years is a long time to go hungry, isn't it, Lindsay?'

'Will you leave my flat or do I have to call the police?' She descended to bluff because she couldn't think of any other way of ending his taunts, she could have kicked herself for giving away the fact that she wasn't sleeping with Aston, it would only make Daniel more sure of himself.

'I'm still waiting for my answer,' he said

without showing any sign of leaving. 'The sooner you agree, the sooner Stephen will be put out of his misery. He must be out of his mind at the moment.'

She closed her eyes, wincing, and knew he was watching her, calculating the effect of what he had just said. Opening her eyes again, she looked at him with a mixture of bitterness and regret. Why was he such a swine? His features held such strength: lean and hard-boned, with that firm jawline and beautifully shaped mouth, those cool, intelligent grey eyes. What sort of mind lay behind them? He was using a cruelly effective blackmail, enlisting her own emotions against her, how could he bring himself to do it?

'You're ruthless, aren't you?' she whispered, and he shrugged.

'If I have to be.'

'Why do you want to humiliate me?' she cried out, her voice shaking, and Daniel's brows jerked together, his features all tightened, his mouth levelling, his cheekbones angular, a tiny muscle jerking beside his mouth.

'If it humiliates you so much, I'm prepared to marry you first,' he said, and laughed, but it was a humourless laughter. 'I know how you insist on that wedding ring,' he added. 'That was what you held out for last time, wasn't it? And you got it, but even that wasn't enough, was it? You still couldn't bear being touched, you bolted. You're a psychological mess, do you know that? When I'm touching you, you burn. It drives me insane to feel that response one minute and the next have you freeze on me and push me away. What happens inside your head to make you ice up like that? Is it guilt? Are you afraid of sex?' His voice held an impassioned pleading now, Lindsay looked at him in shock, her eyes wide. He took a step closer, putting out his hand, and she flinched involuntarily.

'Don't move away from me like that!' Daniel snarled, then he turned away and walked to the door in three strides. 'I said I'd give you until Thursday—I will, but remember, Stephen is waiting for your answer just as much as I am, so don't prolong the agony.'

The front door slammed and Lindsay sank on to the couch, trembling, her thoughts in chaos. Daniel had come strangely close to the truth in his accusation that she was afraid of sex, but it wasn't sex she feared, it was love. Sex was merely the symptom of the disease, love was the sickness itself. Her love for Daniel had been too intense, too devouring: she hadn't been able to control it, she had wanted him too much, been jealous of everyone who came near him, and her jealousy had taken over her whole life in the end, she hadn't slept, hadn't thought about anything else, it had been a permanent torture.

She had thought Daniel knew. Had he forgotten her constant probing, her questions about what he had done, where he had been and with whom? She had thought she was so obvious—hadn't he realised, after all?

She sat in the darkening room, a slender white statue on the couch, unmoving. Daniel seemed to see their marriage from an entirely different angle—he remembered everything in a totally different way. But he had one thing right—she was a psychological mess, she couldn't deny that. Her jealousy was a desire for total possession, she had long ago faced that, and that was abnormal; she had had to leave him to escape the endless maze of that bitter, unrewarding emotion. She did not want to be drawn back into it, but if she allowed herself to love Daniel, she was afraid that she would.

CHAPTER EIGHT

'YOU'RE looking rather wan,' Chris told her next morning, eyeing her through half-closed lids as he lounged back in his swivel chair in his favourite position, feet on the desk and arms behind his head.

'The heat,' Lindsay lied, and looked out of the window at the blue, blue sky that floated overhead, unconcerned that London was suffering, far below, from the remorseless heat of the sun. 'Another scorching day,' she added. 'You're lucky I came to work at all, I was thinking of going off to the local swimming pool.'

'Poor little dear,' said Chris, and nudged a pile of reports with one beautifully shod foot. 'Take these and skim through them for me, will you? I'd like a brief résumé by lunchtime.'

'Yes, boss,' she said with venom. 'Anything else I can do?'

'Not just now,' he decided, settling back for a nap with his eyes shut, and she left the office with a crash as the door banged behind her and the glass shook in all the windows on that floor.

'Temper, temper!' Chris yodelled after her.

Her secretary grinned as Lindsay passed her. 'Pleased with himself, today, isn't he?'

'As Punch,' Lindsay agreed, going into her office and dumping the reports on her desk with a groan. That lot would take her all day, Chris could wait for his résumé.

She rang Stephen before she began work on them. Alice answered the phone and told her Stephen had gone to work. 'He insisted, I couldn't persuade him to stay at home any longer.'

'How is he?' Lindsay couldn't get out of her mind the haggard face of her brother last time they met.

'Quiet,' Alice said flatly. 'I think he worries more about the staff at the factory than he does about us, all he keeps saying is: Where will they get other jobs if I have to shut down? He isn't worried about us.'

'Of course he is, you know that isn't true. He was so worried about you that he couldn't face telling you.' Lindsay was indignant on her brother's behalf, Alice was being unfair to him. Lindsay could understand why her sister-in-law was upset, Alice had two small children to think about, she must be very unhappy about losing her home, but that was no reason to be so unkind to Stephen.

'He was so worried about me that he let me go through hell thinking he might be dead,' Alice muttered.

'Oh, Alice!' Lindsay said on a sigh, and heard Alice draw a shaky breath.

'I know,' she said suddenly. 'I'm so angry with him I can't bear it at times, he hurt me, I feel insulted because he didn't confide in me, he rang Aston Hill and he barely knows the man. I feel so small, being left out like that. I'm his wife!'

'Daniel may help him,' Lindsay said on

impulse, and Alice broke into the sentence with an eagerness that hurt.

'Did he tell you that? Do you think he meant it? Has he talked to Stephen?'

'Daniel's cautious, he takes his time to think these things through,' Lindsay told her. 'He won't have talked to Stephen yet, not until he's sure of his plans.'

'It would be marvellous,' said Alice, her voice much lighter now. 'It would take such a load off Stephen, he doesn't know which way to turn.'

Lindsay rang off a moment later and sat staring at the wall. Then she slowly picked up the phone and dialled again, her hand shaking. She found herself counting the rings, and when they stopped and a voice spoke she almost jumped out of her skin.

'I want to speak to Mr Randall,' she said, and the voice took on a tone which had the texture of icecream, frigidly smooth.

'I'll put you through to Mr Randall's secretary.'

Lindsay waited another half a minute, then a woman spoke politely. 'Can I help you?'

'I want to speak to Mr Randall,' Lindsay said again. She hesitated, and before she could decide which name to use the other woman said: 'Who is it speaking, please?' in a distant voice that put her back up so much that she said tersely: 'Mrs Randall.'

There was a silence, then the secretary said: 'Mrs Randall?' again, and Lindsay told her: 'His wife.' When the woman spoke again her voice was very different.

'Would you hold the line for a moment, Mrs Randall? I'll see if I can find Mr Randall, I don't know if he is in his office at the moment.'

Lindsay made grotesque faces at the phone as she waited, and a full minute elapsed before Daniel's voice murmured in her ear.

'Lindsay?'

'Yes,' she said.

He waited, then said: 'What did you want?'

'Yes, I said,' Lindsay muttered, and a long silence fell, then he breathed audibly close to the phone.

'We'd better have lunch today. I'll pick you up outside your office at twelve-thirty.'

'I can't . . .' she began, only to find that he had hung up, the phone had gone dead. Lindsay replaced it, her skin tight around her jaws. She was aching with tension. Did he have to be so brusque? It had cost her a great deal to make that call, he might have been more responsive than that.

She forced herself to turn her attention to work, concentrating on the pile of reports to such an extent that when the door opened she didn't hear it and Chris's voice made her start violently.

'Jumpy today, aren't you?' he observed, staring down at her.

'I was working,' she retorted. 'You could try it, surprise yourself.'

'I'm just off to lunch,' he said, looking amused. 'Coming?'

Lindsay looked at the time, incredulous as she saw that it was twenty to one. 'Oh, no,' she said. 'I'm going to be late.'

He lifted his eyebrows enquiringly. 'Got a date with Aston?'

'No,' she said, unforthcoming. She got up and started towards the door with Chris in hot pursuit. 'I'm going to the cloakroom, where are you off to?' she asked him without turning round.

'Is it a client?' Chris asked, and she ran into the cloakroom, letting the door swing shut in his face without answering.

In front of a mirror she brushed her hair, renewed her make-up and inspected her reflection. She was wearing her white silk blouse with a lightweight green linen skirt tightly belted at the waist with a thin gilt belt. She looked cool and efficient, she did not look exactly sexy, but she decided that that was probably a good thing.

She hadn't escaped from Chris, he was waiting for her at the lift and gave her a beatific grin as she joined him.

'Going my way?'

She walked into the lift and they travelled down together. 'You aren't going to let me expire of curiosity, are you?' Chris asked.

'Definitely,' she told him.

'How can you be so hardhearted?'

'Easily, it's a gift.' The palms of her hands were perspiring, she pulled a tissue out of her bag and wiped them while Chris watched, his face speculative.

'He's obviously someone special,' he guessed aloud. 'You're in quite a state.'

Lindsay walked out of the lift and halted seeing Daniel standing in the foyer talking to a laughing receptionist who was looking at him as if Santa had just delivered him, gift-wrapped. Lindsay had never liked the girl, she decided.

'I'll ring the office,' the receptionist said as Daniel smiled at her. 'She may have left.'

Lindsay started towards the reception desk, her high heels clicking on the stone floor, and Daniel swung in her direction. His grey eyes shot over her and she gave him a curt nod.

'Sorry to keep you waiting, I was delayed.'

He was in a formal, striped suit and crisp white shirt today, his tie a lustrous maroon silk; he looked oddly remote, unfamiliar. His lean, brown face had a controlled smile in it, but the smile did not show in his eyes, they probed her face as though she was an enemy he faced across a minefield. That was how she felt, too. She looked at him coldly because she needed all her armour, all her weapons. This time she was not going to face him empty-handed and already in a losing position.

Daniel glanced past her at Chris, who was hovering behind her shoulder. Lindsay reluctantly introduced them, aware of Chris's curiosity in every nerve, and the two men shook hands. Chris had a coaxing smile on his face, Daniel didn't smile at all, he eyed Chris assessingly from head to foot in one smooth look.

'We must rush, I'm afraid,' he said to him. 'We're late already. Nice to have met you.' Taking Lindsay's elbow, he steered her out of the building and she heard Chris wandering behind them, gloomily guessing that when she got back to work she was going to face a barrage of questions from him. Chris had no sense of shame, if he wanted to know something, he asked and went on asking until he was satisfied.

'Good looking guy,' Daniel said without pleasure, watching her out of the corner of his eye. 'How long have you been working for him?'

'Oh, ages,' Lindsay said blithely.

'You seem to get on well with him.'

'I do,' she said, and halted as she saw the gleaming limousine waiting for them at the kerb with a uniformed chauffeur standing beside it. The man whisked open the passenger door and Daniel slid Lindsay into the car, joining her a second later. Lindsay saw Chris standing on the pavement, watching them in fascination. She resisted the temptation to put her tongue out at him, keeping her profile turned towards him.

'Where are we going?' she asked Daniel. The chauffeur got into the driver's seat and started the engine, the car moved off.

'To have lunch,' he told her with a quick, sideways look. 'You look very businesslike, do you like working at Vivons?'

'Love it.'

'What exactly do you do there?'

'Public relations,' she said. 'Publicity, advertising . . . we all come under the same department and I've worked on all three.'

'Will you be sorry to leave?' He sounded so casual she didn't realise what he had said for a few seconds, then she did a double-take.

'I'm not leaving Vivons.' She sat up, turning to stare fixedly at him. 'No way, don't even think that for a second. I enjoy my job, I'm going to keep it. I'd be bored out of my skull doing nothing all day.'

'Don't get aggressive with *me*,' Daniel muttered, frowning. 'You gave up your job at the bank.'

'Who wouldn't?' Lindsay retorted. 'It was dead boring, but working at Vivons isn't. I'm good at my job and I get a kick out of it.'

'The idea's ridiculous,' he said. 'You won't need a job.'

'Who says I won't? I'll decide what I need.'

'You'll decide?' he echoed slowly, staring at her, the bones in his face locked tight in grim impatience, and Lindsay outfaced him, her eyes defiant.

'That's right. It's my life and my job.' The car was slowing and she looked out of the window vaguely, her mind set on the little argument they had been having, only to jerk awake as she realised where they were. They had entered the curved drive-in of the block of Mayfair flats where Daniel lived, and she flung him a suspicious look.

'What are we doing here?'

'We're having lunch here,' Daniel told her coolly as the limousine stopped. He got out and came round to hand her out of the car. The chauffeur stood there, his face blank, and Lindsay didn't feel like arguing with Daniel in front of him, she had no choice but to allow herself to be led into the building, and he knew she wouldn't be able to do much about it. He had kept her mind on their row while they drove here, looking back she suspected that he had deliberately trailed his coat for her to pounce on—he was a devious swine.

In the lift she turned on him, her hands curled into fists at her sides, anger flaring in her green eyes. 'You knew I thought we were going to a restaurant! You deliberately didn't tell me you were bringing me here.'

'That's right,' he agreed lazily. 'You wouldn't have come otherwise.'

'You . . .' Words jammed her mind as she tried to find a description vivid enough to make clear how she felt about him, she looked at him in helpless, seething fury, and he laughed.

The lift doors slid open and Daniel took her arm and half led, half thrust her towards the front door of his flat. He had two homes in London, this spacious penthouse flat where he lived himself and a house a quarter of a mile away where his mother lived but where he often stayed, usually when he was entertaining visitors, since the house had far more room. The flat only had three bedrooms, and was a short walk from Daniel's office headquarters, so that he could be immediately available night or day in a business crisis.

Halting at the door, he glanced down at her with mockery in his smile. 'Try to look pleasant for Mrs Henshaw.'

Lindsay opened her mouth to answer that and he put a hand over her lips. 'No backchat,' he warned, and she felt like biting the hand, then he took it away and rang the bell. The door was whisked open and Mrs Henshaw stood there, smiling.

'Oh, Mrs Randall, it's good to see you. How are you? You look very well.'

'I'm fine,' said Lindsay, smiling back. Mrs Henshaw was a short, thin, neat woman with a slightly harassed expression at times and pale blue eyes that dominated her otherwise un-memorable face. They were protuberant, enormous, always glazed as though she might be going to cry. 'How are you, Mrs Henshaw?' Lindsay asked her, and the other woman shrugged cheerfully.

'Mustn't grumble.'

It was embarrassing to face her; Mrs Henshaw had been an onlooker during the months when Lindsay was left alone night after night while Daniel was supposedly working. The other woman must know far too much about Daniel's private life, Lindsay was uneasy with her, and she sensed uneasiness in Mrs Henshaw, too.

'We'll have lunch whenever you're ready, Mrs Henshaw,' said Daniel, moving away, and the housekeeper gave Lindsay an odd look, saying: 'Mr Randall, could I have a word?'

'Problems?' Daniel asked, half-smiling. 'Don't tell me you've ruined our lunch?' He was looking amused as he waited, but Mrs Henshaw's expression was agitated.

'Oh, sir, it wasn't my fault, I didn't know what to do . . .' Her nervous words stopped dead as a door opened and out strolled the blonde Lindsay had seen with Daniel the other night.

'I thought I heard your voice,' she purred, and linked her arms round Daniel's neck, smiling into his eyes. 'I just had to talk to you, darling.' She appeared not to notice Lindsay, she ignored Mrs Henshaw, all her attention on Daniel. She put on a good act, Lindsay thought sourly: lashes fluttering, her full pink mouth lifted as though for a kiss, the lipstick moist and glowing, her body deliberately arched against him.

'What's the matter, Carolyn?' Daniel asked coolly, his hands going up to unlock her arms and pull them down.

'I'm not happy,' the blonde told him, pouting. 'A promise is a promise—you can't say you didn't give me your word I'd get everything I want, but now Harry tells me your people are being awkward.' She came just up to his shoulder; a tiny, curved creature whose every movement shouted sex appeal, and Daniel looked at her with amused indulgence.

'Mrs Henshaw, would you give Mrs Randall a drink? I won't be a moment.' He put his arm around the girl's waist and walked her away to the room he used as a study. Lindsay watched, her teeth meeting. Somehow she hung on to her smile, she wasn't going to let Mrs Henshaw see her real feelings. She walked into the room which the blonde had emerged from, her head held high and her expression unconcerned, aware of the housekeeper scurrying at her heels.

'What can I get you, Mrs Randall? Will you have a sherry?'

'That would be nice,' said Lindsay sitting down in one of the deep, smoothly upholstered chairs. The room had been newly decorated, and recently; she had a shock as she realised that, she had expected it to look exactly the same, and finding that it didn't was disorientating. The furniture was all covered in blue suede, the material clung softly to her hands as she touched it, the feel of it sensuous. The carpet was new, too, a deep-piled white on which were laid some Persian rugs whose colours glowed vividly; red and green and blue.

'Sweet or dry?' Mrs Henshaw asked, and Lindsay told her: 'Sweet,' smiling politely. She was feeling numb, it was stupid to feel hurt because Daniel had redecorated the home they had shared together. What had she expected? That he would keep it exactly the same? Reason told her she was being stupid, but she resented it, she felt he had betrayed her all over again by altering their home.

Mrs Henshaw handed her a delicate glass of warm, golden sherry and hovered. Didn't she like to leave Lindsay alone? Or was she trying to say something? Lindsay pretended not to notice her, she sipped her sherry, her eyes lowered.

'If you want anything ...' Mrs Henshaw mumbled, and Lindsay looked up, nodded.

'Thank you.'

Mrs Henshaw went out and Lindsay looked around the room taking in everything, recognising nothing. What had he wanted to do? Erase all memory of her?

The door opened and Daniel came in, wariness in his face. 'Sorry about that,' he said quickly, his glance skimming across the room towards her.

'I'm sure you are,' Lindsay smiled, ice in her eyes.

'She was uptight about the contract she's signing with us,' he said, pretending not to notice the glacial nature of the smile.

'Just business?' she asked, her tone sarcastic. 'It looked pretty personal to me.'

'Carolyn calls everyone darling,' he shrugged, getting himself a glass of whisky. 'She's an uninhibited girl.'

'So I noticed, she must be very popular.' With men, Lindsay added mentally; the blonde girl had apparently found other women invisible, she hadn't so much as glanced in Lindsay's direction.

Daniel turned, smiling drily. 'I must be crazy,' he said, looking at her with raised brows, 'getting involved with you again—red hair, green eyes, a temper like blazing oil, and a nasty, suspicious little mind.'

'I didn't imagine the way she hung on your neck and oozed sex appeal,' Lindsay snapped, then thought back over what he had just said and added tersely: 'And nobody asked you to get involved with me again.'

He drank some whisky, watching her over the glass, his eyes brooding. 'When I eat lobster I come out in a rash,' he said irrelevantly, and she stared, lips parted in bafflement, until he added with a wry grimace: 'But I can't resist the stuff, although I know what will happen if I give in to temptation.'

Lindsay coloured, her throat beating with an over-rapid pulse. It wasn't very flattering, being compared to lobster, but what he had actually said hadn't mattered so much as the dark, brooding stare with which he had said it.

He took a step towards her and she shrank, trembling, afraid of the expression in his eyes.

There was a light tap on the door and a second later Mrs Henshaw came in, smiling, to tell them that lunch was ready. Over the meal, Lindsay asked Daniel: 'Have you talked to Stephen yet?' and he nodded.

'It's all settled. I'm becoming his partner, he'll still be running the factory, but he'll be answerable to me. My people will work out the details. I'll put somebody in there to work with Stephen, my accountants insist on that, we're investing a lot of money and they want safeguards.' He gave her a brief, dry smile. 'But your brother's pride won't suffer too much, I promise you. Anyone who bailed him out would insist on similar terms.'

Lindsay kept her eyes on the plate in front of her, she was having trouble eating the delicately flavoured Chicken Bretagne which Mrs Henshaw had served with saffron rice and fresh peas. It was a dish which Lindsay had always liked; Mrs Henshaw's memory was good.

'Have you told Stephen ...' she began, faltered, then added: 'That I ...' And broke off again, unable to think of a way of phrasing it.

'That you're coming back to me?' Daniel asked softly, and she felt his eyes on her flushed face. 'No,' he said. 'I thought we would be subtle about that, it might look suspicious if the two pieces of news came together. We'll wait a week or two before we tell him, I think.'

'How tactful,' Lindsay said bitterly. 'Is that for your sake or mine? Stephen might be angry if he knew how you'd blackmailed me.'

'He's stiff-necked,' Daniel said. 'I'm sure he'd

refuse my help if he found out.' His voice taunted her. 'Of course, if you choose to tell him . . .'

'No!' she exclaimed with violence.

'Somehow I thought you wouldn't,' Daniel murmured.

'That's what you're relying on,' she flung back at him. 'You wouldn't want anyone to know how low you'd stoop and you're banking on the fact that I'd hate my brother to know what you've forced me to do!'

'Everything has its price,' he said, his voice cool, but there was nothing cool about his eyes, they glinted like hot metal, because he had not liked what she said, he hadn't liked the voice she used as she said it. Daniel might be using blackmail remorselessly, but he did not want her to keep underlining that fact. He preferred the truth kept out of sight.

'Our deal is just between the two of us,' he said. 'Nobody else is involved.' He watched her, his fingers curled around his wine-glass, their tips lightly tapping the stem of the glass. 'And that includes Aston Hill.'

'I don't intend to tell Aston! I'd hate him to know, too. He would be horrified, I'd feel sick if I had to tell him.'

Daniel frowned, his mouth straight, dark red running along his cheekbones. Lindsay kept her eyes on him, hoping her pointed remarks were making him angry. She wanted to hurt him, to prick that thick skin of his, she was still raw from the memory of seeing the blonde actress hanging round his neck and calling him 'darling' in those honeyed tones. Last time she had run away because loving him hurt so much, and she couldn't live in a ceaseless atmosphere of doubt and jealousy. Nothing had changed, Daniel was still the same man, she had to be stupid to let history repeat itself. Somehow she had to keep a wall between them, she had to learn not to care what he did, who he was with, how he felt. During their separation she had built up a satisfactory life of her own, she had learnt so much about herself and about life since she left him and she was determined not to make the mistake of letting her emotions take control of her, not this time. She would just have to keep him at arms' length.

Mrs Henshaw served their coffee and Lindsay glanced at her watch. 'Look at the time! I'll have to be going soon—I've got a mountain of work to get through before I can leave tonight.'

'Drink your coffee and I'll drive you back to your office.' Daniel looked at his own watch, shrugging. 'I'll have to get back to work myself.'

In the car, he asked: 'Dinner tonight?' and Lindsay shook her head.

'I'm having dinner with Aston.'

She felt him stiffen. When he spoke again his voice held a muffled snarl of temper. 'That's over now, you know that? You're not dating him again. We're getting remarried, the press would have a field day if you were seen with another man.'

He couldn't speak too loudly because he was afraid the chauffeur would hear him. Lindsay gave him a sweet smile. 'Aston's an old friend.' The car had stopped, she opened the door and quickly fled before she got any reaction from Daniel.

Of course, Chris was waiting for her, buzzing with questions. She regarded him wryly. 'Oh, well, you might as well know—we're getting married again.'

His jaw dropped. 'You and Daniel Randall . . .'

'Me and Daniel Randall,' she nodded. 'Happy now? Can I do some work?'

'When?' Chris demanded, and she looked at her piled desk.

'Now might be a good time before I get buried alive in paper.'

'No,' he said impatiently. 'When are you getting married again?' Then he laughed and said: 'You knew what I meant.'

'In a fortnight,' Lindsay told him. 'We just spent an hour planning it—that gives his damned sister time to buy a new hat, let's hope it hides her face.' Daniel's sister had never liked Lindsay. Meriel was a feline, self-important woman with too much money, too much time on her hands and too little to do with either.

Chris stared at her, wide awake for once. 'I didn't know you were still seeing him,' he said slowly. 'I thought it was Aston . . .'

Lindsay shrugged and couldn't think of an answer for that. Chris ran a hand through his glowing, honey-blond hair, frowning.

'I hope you'll be happy,' he said in a dubious way, looking distinctly worried, then he wandered away and Lindsay sat looking at nothing. So did she, wasn't that what everyone wanted? To be happy? Marriage to Daniel Randall didn't seem a likely prospect for finding happiness, though. Heartache, perhaps, she had had enough of that last time, he was good at that.

She got home late that evening and had to rush to shower and change before Aston arrived. She was just brushing a little rouge along her cheekbones when the doorbell went. She ran to open it, smiling, but it wasn't Aston, it was a girl in a T-shirt and jeans who grinned at her and handed her the enormous cellophane-wrapped bouquet she was holding.

'Mrs Randall?'

'Yes.' Lindsay said. 'Thank you.'

They were beautiful. She walked slowly into the kitchen cradling them, deep red velvety roses with long stems, frilly white carnations, yellow gladioli. Lindsay stripped off the cellophane and began to put them in vases. The doorbell went again and this time it was Aston. He looked at the rose she held, smiling.

'For me?' he asked, his mouth crooked.

She laughed, walking back into the kitchen. He stood at her shoulder, staring at the flowers, watching her finish the arrangement.

'Randall?' His voice was quiet, it held no particular intonation.

She nodded without looking round, nerving herself to tell him she was remarrying Daniel, but before she could say anything, Aston's hands gripped her shoulders, he moved closer, his mouth moving against her neck.

'He's chasing you again, isn't he, Lindsay?' She felt the pressure of his lips, heard him breathing quickly. 'Don't let him too near you, have you forgotten what he did to you last time? It was a year before you could bear a man near you, you were a human iceberg.' His hands slid down her arms and round her waist, she felt them warm and firm below her breasts. 'I've waited too long,' he said unsteadily, and she was disturbed by the note in his voice. 'I should have turned a blow-torch on you long ago.'

'Aston——' she began, but he was spinning her round to face him and as she looked up into the rugged, humorous face she saw a new expression, one she had never seen before; a fierce excitement, a passion, that silenced her in shock.

His arms went round her, pulled her close in a convulsive, demanding movement, and he kissed her hungrily, with desire, with pleading, and the sheer naked need in that kiss sent her spinning off balance, everything female in her responded to Aston's unhidden need of her. He pressed her even closer, a hand gripping her back, and his mouth was warm and sensuous. He had never kissed her like this before, and she yielded to him without being able to think.

It was always dangerous to think you knew someone, she thought; had she been so wrong about Aston? Her heart was going inside her like a steam-hammer, crashing wildly, she couldn't breathe. Aston was turning her body to soft, yielding wax in his caressing hands.

He lifted his head, breathing raggedly. Lindsay opened her eyes, dazed by the light, and he said in a husky voice: 'I love you.'

She burst into tears.

CHAPTER NINE

'DARLING!' Aston sounded horrified. He tipped up her face and gently wiped her eyes with a hankie, murmuring soothingly: 'What is it? Lindsay darling, don't, I didn't mean to frighten you—don't cry, love.'

She couldn't stop the tears, they poured out of her like Niagara Falls, she rubbed her hand across her wet face and Aston said: 'You're smudging your mascara, you look like a panda,' which made her giggle hysterically and then hiccup, crying and laughing together.

Aston urged her into the sitting-room, pushed her down on the couch. 'What you need is a drink,' he said. 'I need one myself,' he added in a self-mocking voice. 'A stiff whisky, that's what I need. I seem to have rubber legs.' He went over to pour the drinks, saying with his back to her: 'That was some kiss.' He sounded selfconscious; he was not given to such violent emotion, he was a calm man who liked his life to be under control. Lindsay had never expected him to break out like that, she had thought she had him worked out to the last detail, she had been wrong, and she was dreading the next few moments. How was she going to tell him about Daniel now?

She hadn't expected Aston to be pleased, of course, she had known he would be taken aback, even hurt or angry, but it hadn't entered her head that under his smiling surface there lurked such strong feelings.

He came over and put a glass into her hand, sat down next to her, swallowing some of the whisky in his own glass. He was very flushed, he looked like a man who has surprised himself and isn't sure what to do next. Lindsay glanced at him secretly from under her lashes, pretending to sip her whisky. Grimacing at the taste, she said huskily: 'Aston, I've got to tell you . . .'

'I know,' he said, interrupting. 'Why do you think I haven't rushed you until now? I knew you weren't in love with me, I realised I had to be patient. Don't think I'm expecting an answer right away, I just wanted you to know how I felt.' He blushed and looked down into his whisky, smiling, a quick, secret smile he tried to hide by turning his head away, but too late, Lindsay had seen it. 'I should have shown you sooner,' he said, and she knew from that smile that her response to his passionate kiss had misled him into thinking she felt more for him than she did.

Or was he right? She sat up, jerked into cold self-appraisal. How had she felt? At the time she had been swept away like a straw on a flooding river, helpless to do more than go with the compelling tide. She hadn't been thinking or assessing how she felt, she had given in to him mindlessly. If Daniel had not come back into her life, would she have fallen in love with Aston, sooner or later? She had been telling herself she liked him but nothing more; she had seen him in a different light now and she was no longer so sure.

What was love, anyway? Why did she feel the way she did about Daniel, rather than any other man? His looks? Other men were as good-looking, but they didn't do a thing to her heartbeat. His wealth and power? If he had been as rich as Croesus but hadn't turned her on, she wouldn't have looked at him twice. His personality? She grimaced, drinking some more whisky. Daniel had the personality of a steam-roller; he crushed everyone he met and left them flattened at his feet.

There was a lot of hostility in the way she felt about him, but she couldn't hide from herself the truth that her emotions towards him were complicated, involved, convoluted, like a thick skein of multi-coloured silks, twisted together and almost impossible to unwind without violence. When she was with him she couldn't take her eyes off him, he fascinated her; images flashed through her head now and she felt that betraying weakness she always felt when she was with him. Daniel's wide, firm mouth, smiling, or hard, his lashes lying on his skin like shadows when he looked down, his brown neck, the slow pulse at the base of it, the way he moved suddenly, the long legs graceful. She visualised without thinking, swallowing on a sudden dry-mouthed intensity. How can you pinpoint the focus of so deep an attraction? Perhaps it was none of those things, perhaps it was in herself that she should be looking—her own nature needed something she sensed in Daniel and not in any other man, but she didn't have a clue what it was she needed.

Would she have found it with Aston, though?

She looked at him and he was watching her, his mouth crooked.

'Don't look so worried, it will wait,' he said, and she wanted to cry again because *he* was trying to comfort *her* and that made her ache with guilt.

Self-hatred forced the words out of her. 'I'm going to marry Daniel.'

Aston sat there, staring at her, his glass clutched in his hand. He looked as though he hadn't understood the words. The colour drained slowly out of his face.

'I tried to tell you,' Lindsay mumbled in a low voice.

He leaned over and put down his glass, whisky spilled out of it at the crash as it hit the table.

'Why?'

The word had a raw force behind it. She couldn't meet his eyes, she was pale and she felt sick. What could she tell him? Not the truth, obviously, the situation was explosive enough without that.

'I don't know,' she said helplessly, her lower lip trembling, and in a sense that was the truth, the whole truth and nothing but the truth. On the surface Daniel was blackmailing her, but under that there lay whole layers of reasons for what was happening, subterranean levels of feeling one upon another, so complex she couldn't reach the end of them.

'What do you mean, you don't know?' Aston broke out angrily, and he might well be angry—she knew she sounded fatuous, stupid, she wasn't making sense, to him or herself. 'Are you out of your mind?' he asked, and she grasped almost gratefully at the question.

'Yes,' she said, and began to laugh now, a high-pitched, unbalanced laughter close to tears. 'Stop it!' Aston muttered, and she stopped, dead, swallowing.

'You can't be serious,' he protested. 'After what you've said about him? He's poison to you!'

A sweet poison, Lindsay thought, shuddering, and felt the ache of desire deep inside herself— wasn't that what Daniel had meant when he said that although lobster brought him out in a rash he couldn't resist it? Did he feel the same about her? Were they both aware that it was insanity for them to be together, but far more painful for them to be apart? During their separation she had built up a pleasant life, her days had been busy and painless, her burnt-out nerves had had a chance to heal, she should have been very happy, but since Daniel came back into her world she had felt fifty times more alive, a hundred times more real. He hurt, he drove her crazy, but she needed him.

Aston was looking at her grimly. 'Just now——' he began, and she put her hands over her face. He had good reason to be angry with her, she was angry with herself.

'I'm sorry,' she muttered through her fingers, and he pulled them down, refusing to let her hide from him.

'Why did you let me kiss you like that when all the time you knew you were going to marry Randall again?'

'I didn't mean to ... I'm sorry ... Aston, I like you so much, but ... what can I say? I don't know, you've every right to hate me, I wouldn't blame you if you did, I wish I could love you,

you're a wonderful man.'

He got up in a fierce, aggressive movement. 'I don't want to hear any more. I don't understand you, I don't understand women at all.' He walked to the door and Lindsay sat on the couch, shivering.

Aston stopped at the door, looked back. His hazel eyes were still almost black, his jawline rigid. She thought he was going to say something and waited, not quite meeting that stare, but after a long silence he went without a word, closing the front door very quietly.

Lindsay sat there without moving for a long time, then she got up unsteadily and went into the kitchen, to be met by a wave of perfume from the flowers Daniel had sent her. She looked at them with animosity, as though they were to blame for what had happened. She pulled some of the roses out, water dripping on the floor as she did so, and was barely conscious of the thorns pricking her skin. Half sobbing, she tore the flowers between her fingers. 'Damn you, damn you!' she whispered, and flung them from her. They drifted to the floor in a shower of torn crimson petals and green leaves. Her fingers showed tiny spots of blood, she stared at them with clouded eyes. He was hurting her already.

The phone rang, making her jump. She answered it reluctantly. It was Stephen, sounding almost lightheaded. 'I suppose you know,' he said, and she pretended not to understand, her voice puzzled. 'Know what?'

'You don't?' Stephen sounded disbelieving, but he told her about Daniel's offer and she exclaimed joyfully, hoping she wasn't over-acting and that he wouldn't guess she knew all about it.

'Isn't that wonderful? I'm so glad—are you pleased? Is he giving you a good deal, or aren't you happy with his offer?'

'He's being more than handsome,' Stephen told her in a slightly dry tone. 'I'd be an ungrateful fool if I wasn't relieved and delighted. Nobody loses their job, the firm stays nominally mine and Alice won't have to leave her house. I couldn't in my wildest dreams have hoped for anything like Daniel's offer.' He talked about the details for a while, then said: 'Thanks, Lindsay,' and she protested: 'What for, what did I do? I had nothing to do with it.'

'Pull the other one,' Stephen said bluntly. 'Daniel Randall isn't the quixotic type, he and I were never that close, he wouldn't do this for me. There's only one person who could get him to play Sir Galahad. He was always nuts about you.'

When she had rung off Lindsay slowly went into her bedroom and sat down on the bed, staring at her own reflection with searching eyes. Her skin had a betraying pallor, her green eyes looked too large, too bright, their lids flickering nervously as she stared at herself and saw in the mirror those hints of emotional turmoil which she did not want anyone else to glimpse. She ran a shaky hand through her hair and it flamed in the lamplight, soft, gleaming red curls which clung to her pale fingers. She thought of Daniel, and involuntarily, her eyes shut, she breathed faster, hating herself but wanting him. If only she knew how he felt about her—did he hate her? She knew he desired her, but how much of that desire was hatred?

It's so easy, she thought, to hate and love at one and the same time, the piercing emotional intensity of both can be mistaken for the other.

She undressed and slipped into bed, turned out the light and tried to sleep. She was very tired, sleep should have come quickly, but it evaded her. It was some time before she felt her body relaxing and then just as she was falling asleep the phone rang. Groggily, she groped for it in the dark and the bedside lamp almost crashed to the floor. She lifted the phone and mumbled: 'Mmm ...' Even as she muttered that she was waking up and guessing that Aston had rung, her face wary as she finally managed to find the lamp switch and turn on the light.

'Lindsay?' The voice was hard and cool and it wasn't Aston's—it was Daniel, sounding distinctly harsh.

'What on earth ...' She looked at her bedside clock in disbelief. 'Do you know what time it is? It's midnight.' Then fear made her voice rise. 'What's wrong?' Her mind leapt to the obvious. 'Stephen ...'

'Is fine, as far as I know,' said Daniel. 'I was ringing to make sure you were okay.'

'You were what? You wake me up to ... I don't believe my ears!'

'I just saw Hill,' he said tersely.

Lindsay froze. 'What? Aston? Where? What did ...'

'We didn't speak,' Daniel said. 'He was drunk. It was the most incredible thing—I was with a party of Swedes over here on a buying expedition, we'd been having dinner and went on to a club. Hill was going out as we went in—he saw me, gave me one look and hit me.'

Lindsay's breathing seemed to stop. She gripped the phone tighter.

'Luckily he was too drunk to connect,' Daniel told her. 'I was his fist coming, side-stepped, and he fell flat on his face.'

'Oh, no!' Lindsay gasped. 'Poor Aston . . . is he hurt?'

'Providence looks after drunks,' said Daniel without apparent sympathy. 'He passed out, but I didn't see any injuries, and luckily my Swedish friends took it as a joke, they thought he'd taken an instant dislike to me because he was stoned.'

'Where is he now?'

'Home, I'd imagine—I called my driver over and sent him home in my car.' He paused. 'Then I rang you to make sure you were safely home. You told him, I presume?'

'Yes,' she said very quietly.

'Took it badly, did he?'

'Damn you,' Lindsay muttered, her voice shaking. 'Mind your own business!'

'Was there a scene?' Daniel asked. 'He didn't hurt you, did he?' He sounded icily harsh, and she hated him.

'Go to hell,' she said, and hung up. She crawled down into the bed and pulled the sheet over her head, but although she kept her eyes tightly shut she could not shut out the pictures Daniel had conjured up for her. Poor Aston! She hated herself, she hated Daniel, and most of all she hated knowing that she had hurt Aston so much that he had gone off to drink himself insensible. She knew how he felt, she wished she could do the same, but she would only be sick if she tried to drink enough to stop her mind from working.

She closed her hands around her head, rocking to and fro in the bed on her knees, like a demented woman. Her mind was her real problem, it wouldn't stop working, telling her home truths she didn't want to hear. Her body was always on Daniel's side—if her mind would only stop interfering, she could forget pain, give in to the heated necessity in her flesh and be oblivious of everything else. She felt like banging her head on a wall until her mind gave up.

Over the next few days she was grateful for the fact that she was too busy to have time to think. The office was hectic, Chris even did some work himself, but he did so with more vigour when the managing director was around. Charles rarely appeared on their floor, he normally summoned Chris to his own much plushier suite, but he was taking a great interest in their campaign to find 'The Face'. Chris's original brainwave had been enlarged—they were launching their new range at the same time as their highly publicised competition to find the perfect girl to represent Vivons, and both newspaper and television advertisements would feature a large cut-out silhouette of a girl's head without features, only a question mark and the words: Are You The Face?

'Clever,' said Charles, nodding approval. He looked at Lindsay. 'He's a genius, isn't he?'

'A genius,' Lindsay agreed, but when he had gone she eyed Chris with wry amusement. 'Stop preening, you look like a half-witted peacock!'

He laughed, then looked at her hard. 'And you look like a ghost—not sleeping? You haven't looked too good all week. Does Daniel Randall keep you awake all night? All play and no work, remember.'

'I work,' Lindsay said. 'A damned sight harder than you . . .'

'It was a joke, a joke,' Chris protested, pretending to be alarmed, holding up both hands as though she might hit him.

'Not a very funny one,' she told him, and he sighed and hung his head.

'No, ma'am, sorry, ma'am, I beg your pardon, ma'am.'

'Oh, get lost,' Lindsay said without heat, and stormed off back to her own office to regret losing her temper over nothing. What was the matter with her? As if she didn't know!

That evening she called in to see Alice and found her very busy cooking Stephen's dinner while Matt and Vicky called plaintively down the stairs for drinks of water. 'They ought to be asleep,' Alice said distractedly, tasting the home-made chicken soup and hesitating about the flavour. 'Is there enough salt in that?' she asked, and Lindsay lifted the ladle and sipped, nodding.

'Plenty, it's delicious.'

'I used the carcase,' said Alice, replacing the saucepan lid. 'Why don't you stay? There's more than enough for three.'

'I'd have loved to, but . . .'

'Date?' Alice asked, and Lindsay nodded, smiling at her, although it was a lie, she didn't have a date, she was simply afraid to talk to her brother for long in case she said too much about Daniel.

'Aston, I suppose?' Alice asked, and Lindsay hesitated, biting her lip.

'Well, no.' Matt's footsteps padded down the stairs and Alice made a wrathful face.

'Back to bed,' she yelled, then looked at Lindsay curiously. 'Who are you seeing tonight?' Her face brightened. 'Daniel?' She stared hard, smiling. 'It is, isn't it? I knew it, I told Stephen so, I guessed from the minute he walked in here that night. If he wasn't still mad about you, he wouldn't have hared over here the minute that reporter told him you were in trouble.'

'Mummy,' Matt said at the door, 'can we . . .'

'I thought I told you to stay in bed? Do you want a smack?'

'No,' said Matt, not surprisingly. He advanced to twine himself round Lindsay's leg, hugging her waist. 'Auntie, tell us a story. We're not sleepy, come and tell us a story, we like your stories, you haven't told us one for ages and ages.'

Lindsay hoisted him up, groaning exaggeratedly. 'Heavens, you're getting heavy! What does your mummy feed you on? Elephant steaks?'

'Take no notice of him,' Alice said crossly. 'He should be asleep, they both should. I put them to bed dead on six, it gets later every night. I can't wait for the autumn, these summer evenings drag on and on.'

'Just a quick story, then,' said Lindsay,

carrying Matt up the stairs. 'I've got to rush, you know, I didn't come round to tell you two stories.' She slid him into his bed and Vicky peered at her through the cot bars, her nose pink in the half-light. Lindsay bent to kiss her on it and Vicky wriggled, chuckling. Lindsay got her to lie down, tucked the cover over her and sat on Matt's bed while she told them a slow version of The Three Bears. Vicky sucked her thumb, eyes half shut. She was quite ready to go off to sleep, it was Matt who was keeping her awake.

When Lindsay got back downstairs Stephen was in the kitchen, sipping a glass of gin and tonic which Alice had given him. He grinned at her. 'Kids asleep?'

'Vicky is—Matt is still full of beans. It's time he had a room of his own, isn't it?'

'You may be right,' said Alice, nodding. 'Drink, Lindsay?'

'No, I must go. See you both soon.' As she walked away Stephen said: 'I'll give you a lift home,' and although she tried to refuse he insisted. 'It won't take me ten minutes,' he said, and Alice joined him in persuading Lindsay to agree. It was obvious that Stephen wanted to talk about Daniel, and Lindsay was reluctant to do that, but she had no choice but to give in to their combined pressure. At the moment, Daniel was their favourite person, Stephen knew how much he owed Daniel and he wanted to impress on his sister that Daniel was a terrific guy. It wasn't selfish of him, it was only human. Stephen had been overwhelmed by Daniel's rescue operation and he wanted to show his appreciation. He thought Daniel was doing it for Lindsay's sake and Stephen was very fond of his sister, he would do a lot for her himself. He already had, Stephen was an unselfish, loving man with a strong sense of family and a deep sense of responsibility. He had placed his own interpretation on what Daniel was doing. Stephen knew that in Daniel's place he would be acting out of love, and it had made it much easier for Stephen to accept Daniel's help since he worked out why Daniel was doing it. He wanted Lindsay to be kind to Daniel, he made that as clear as crystal.

'I feel as if a great load was off my mind,' he told her as he drove her back to her flat. 'It was unbearable, knowing there was no way out. I've never felt so desperate in my life. I was going crazy!'

She listened, her face sombre. 'I'm glad things have worked out,' she said, and Stephen quickly said: 'Thanks to Daniel, he's being terrific. He's already paid off the bank, and his accountants are working to get the business back on a good footing.'

'You will be careful,' Lindsay said hesitantly. 'Daniel is a tough businessman, he'll expect a profit.'

'I want the firm to be profitable,' Stephen told her. 'It has to sell what it makes. I'm not a fool, Lindsay, I'd have let him have the whole firm for a song just to keep the factory open. We were right down the drain, I hadn't got a hope, and all those men and women would have been out of a job. I felt so guilty about them, about Alice and the kids ... it was my fault. I overreached myself, tried to expand too fast, borrowed too much money and then couldn't pay it back—I meant well, but that's a weak excuse.'

'Don't sell yourself short,' Lindsay said crossly. The car stopped outside the flats and she turned and kissed him lightly. 'You're not a bad brother,' she said with a slightly crooked grin.

Neither of them was over-demonstrative. Stephen grinned and looked uneasy. 'Thanks.' He was a grown man with two children of his own, but for a second or two he looked like a pink schoolboy. Hurriedly he said: 'And thanks for being so good to Alice. She was worried sick, I know. I wish to heaven I hadn't put her through that—believe me, I wasn't myself, I'd never have done that to her otherwise.'

'She knows that, we both do.' Lindsay gave him a little punch, smiling. 'So stop apologising, buster. You don't need to, nobody blames you.'

'I do,' Stephen said soberly. 'Alice was as mad as hell for a while, but she's come out of that now. I should have told her—she's right. I just wanted to protect her, I wasn't trying to insult her by keeping her in the dark. I'll never keep anything from her again.' He gave Lindsay a wry grin. 'I didn't know Alice could be so belligerent—she threw things at me, imagine that! I was dumbfounded. Alice! She never even raised her voice to me before.'

Lindsay laughed. 'It sounds as though your marriage is going to be more exciting in future! Let's hope she doesn't take boxing lessons, that's all.' She got out of the car and waved to him as he drove away, then went into the building slowly.

She was tired, she would have a bath and an early night. The flat was dark and empty, and she stood in the little corridor listening to the silence, hating it. It was absurd, she could have stayed with Stephen and Alice that evening and relaxed in a warm, family atmosphere, but she had insisted on coming back here to be alone and now she was feeling lonely and abandoned, she was wallowing in self-pity. How stupid could you get?

She had her bath, soaking herself in warm, luxurious water generously sprinkled with rose-scented bath crystals, lying back listening to the radio with closed eyes, occasionally wiggling a foot to make the water swish around her body, and now and then sipping a glass of Martini. She wasn't in a hurry, she had nowhere to go.

It wasn't until the water was almost cold that she reluctantly stepped out of the bath, dried herself lightly and slid into a robe. She rubbed the mist off the steamy mirror, and peered at her reflection; she looked pink and clean, her red hair curling in the steam, her eyelashes clustered damply. Making a disgusted face at herself, she wandered off to the kitchen to get herself a snack. She looked into the fridge and didn't fancy anything she saw. In the end she fell back on scrambled eggs and toast, but just as she was beating the eggs with a fork the doorbell rang and her hand jerked in surprise.

Aston? She hesitated, biting her lip, not sure if she felt up to facing him tonight, and while she stood there trying to make up her mind the bell rang again with a sharp, peremptory note. Clutching the lapels of her terry-towelling robe, she opened the front door a fraction, looking through the gap warily. Daniel looked back at her, his mouth indented impatiently. He didn't say anything and after a moment Lindsay fell back and let him walk into the flat. She closed the door and leaned on it weakly, her pulses accelerating.

The cold, empty flat was suddenly alive; she was alive, too. Daniel stared at her and smiled suddenly in a way that made her tremble, and then sent a wave of pure rage through her at her own folly. He was looking pleased with himself, his eyes touched her, lingering, and she knew what he was thinking, there was a quality of satisfaction, complacency, in that smile. He thought he had got her, in a moment he was going to kiss her, his lean body was poised to make a move, and she resented every inch of him.

'I'm tired,' she said coldly. 'I've had a difficult day and I'm in no mood to deal with you, Daniel, so whatever you've got to say, say it and go, please.'

He lost the smile and the grey eyes cooled and hardened; anger came from him in icy waves. 'Don't talk to me like that! I won't stand for it!'

Lindsay dug her hands into her robe pockets, hunching her slender shoulders in a shrug, angrily enjoying the new tension in his face. He had come here tonight with one thing on his mind; she had known that the minute she set eyes on him, but he could think again, she wasn't going to be the push-over he expected. She had some self-respect—not much, she thought grimly, but some!

'If it isn't important, could it wait? Ring me tomorrow,' she said, calmly opening the door.

Daniel charged towards it, his wide shoulders tense under the smooth grey suit he wore, his face harsh, every line of it set fiercely in rage. Lindsay hurriedly got out of his way; she had the feeling he might knock her down and trample on her if she didn't.

The door slammed with a violence that made the flat echo, but Daniel hadn't left, he was still on her side of that door, and Lindsay gulped in alarm as he turned a menacing glare on her.

'Now!' he said without any hint of a smile anywhere, and her heart dived down with sickening dismay as he moved towards her.

CHAPTER TEN

'KEEP your hands off me,' she stammered, backing against the wall and Daniel advanced remorselessly, pinning her into the corner. He put a hand on either side of her, his face inches away, a grim, shadowy mask she watched nervously, her eyes very wide and alert to every move he made. She wasn't expecting what he did say, it took her totally by surprise.

'Why did you leave me?' The question had explosive force in it, his voice was harsh, he held her stare fixedly, refusing to let her look away.

'I . . . I'm not going over old history,' Lindsay said in a shaky little voice, wishing he wouldn't stand so close, his nearness was doing drastic things to her heartbeat.

'Oh, yes,' he said, 'you are. I want to know.'

'Too bad,' she muttered, looking down to escape that hypnotic stare and his hand came up to grab her chin and force her face upwards. Her lashes flickered uneasily, she moistened her dry mouth with her tongue-tip. 'If you manhandle me . . .' she began, and Daniel laughed shortly.

'What will you do, Lindsay? Hit me? I told you what would happen if you ever hit me again.'

'Oh, you'd like that, wouldn't you? That turns you on, does it? I didn't have you down as a man who got his kicks from hitting women, but it figures. Force is all you understand!'

'I sure as hell don't understand you,' he said bitterly.

'Have you ever tried?' she threw back, and the grey eyes flashed.

'I'm trying now, in case it had escaped your notice.' His hand came down on her wrist, locking it tightly in a vice; he turned and walked into the sitting-room, pulling her after him, struggling to break free. Daniel sat down on the couch and yanked her down to him, she tumbled helplessly across him and before she could sit up his arm clamped over her so that she lay on his lap, her head on the arm of the couch. Her hair escaped from the pins holding it and flew in all directions, a damp sweet-smelling cloud of fiery red-gold, a few strands drifting across her eyes. Daniel brushed them back, she felt his fingertips lightly touch her lids and shivered.

'Try again,' he said softly. 'Why did you leave me?'

'I was sick of sitting around at home while you made it with other women,' Lindsay said viciously, angry again because she knew her body was throbbing with a deep, aroused, erotic heat. Daniel had her at a disadvantage, she couldn't get up, she couldn't get away from his dangerous proximity without a humiliating struggle, and he was far too close, she could feel his body warmth under her back, she could see the faint blue vein in his neck where his blood beat under that brown skin.

His brows came together. 'What?'

'Did you think I wouldn't guess what kept you out so late night after night?' She sneered, laughing angrily. 'I may have been young, but I wasn't that stupid!'

'I was working,' he said, staring at her, and she laughed again without any humour.

'Oh, sure. And I bet you worked hard, too.'

Daniel was staring at her as though he didn't know her, and she wasn't surprised; she didn't know herself, her jealousy was blackening everything she saw, her face was hot with rage and her voice had the sting of a scorpion. She had hidden her jealousy for so long, now that it was escaping she couldn't control it.

'You thought I had other women?' Daniel sounded incredulous, if she hadn't known better she would have thought his blank expression held innocence, but she did know better. He was acting and doing it brilliantly, but he couldn't fool her.

'I didn't just think,' she said bitingly. 'I knew! Someone was getting your attention, it certainly wasn't me. When we first got married you made love to me every night, then everything changed—some weeks you didn't even kiss me, let alone make love to me! I might as well have been a piece of furniture for all the notice you took.'

'You never said a word,' he protested. 'You didn't tell me you suspected I was having an affair.'

Lindsay curled an icy smile at him. 'Where was the point? You'd either have lied or admitted it—either way, I didn't want to get into that sort of discussion. I was humiliated enough already.'

'So you were judge and jury, you found me guilty without even telling me what I was supposed to be guilty of . . .' He sounded hoarse, little spots of dark red had come up in his face and his mouth was unsteady. Lindsay felt nervous as she looked up at him, she shifted uneasily.

'You stupid brat,' Daniel muttered, and his hand shot out to curl round her throat. She tensed, her nerves jumping with fear. 'I ought to . . .' He broke off again, swallowing, she saw his throat move convulsively. 'Not even to ask me! My word, your opinion of me must have been rock bottom! You couldn't even be bothered to talk about it, you went around secretly accusing me and didn't utter a syllable.' His hand tightened and she flinched. He saw the fear in her face and his lips drew back from his teeth in a snarl. 'Yes, you're right to look nervous! The way I feel at the moment I might just lose my temper and give you what you deserve!'

'Don't threaten me,' Lindsay said as firmly as she could. 'You're not frightening me.' She was lying, he *was* frightening her, but she was not going to admit that even if he had already realised it.

'Then you're even more stupid than I thought,' Daniel muttered. 'You ought to be scared, you're very close to being strangled.' The long fingers flexed on her throat, making her even more aware of their power. 'Who did you think I was seeing? Or didn't that interest you?'

'You had plenty of casual girl-friends before you met me,' Lindsay said with a pretence of cold indifference. 'You told me as much yourself, you never hid your past love life—I knew you used to pick girls up all the time, look at the way you picked me up. Old habits die hard, don't they say?'

He said something she didn't hear, the words choked.

'You can't deny it,' she persisted. 'I wasn't your usual type, was I? You went for more sophisticated ladies and your interest in them wasn't limited to giving them dinner or a night at the theatre. Well, go on—deny you slept with them!'

'Why should I?' he said angrily. 'I was free, adult and normal—why shouldn't I go to bed with an attractive woman if she was willing? But that was before I married you, you aren't accusing me over the distant past. If you thought I was carrying on like that after we were married, why didn't you come out with it? Why hug it to yourself without a word?' He bent down towards her and she shrank, a hand up to keep him at bay. 'Unless, of course, you were looking for an excuse to leave me!'

Her flush deepened. 'That's right, make a counter-accusation! I didn't need an excuse, you handed me a reason on a plate.'

'I didn't do anything of the kind! There were no other women,' he said, and she smiled, angrily incredulous.

'No?'

'I'll make you believe me if I have to beat you black and blue,' he muttered, and took hold of her shoulders, twisting her forcibly while she struggled and kicked, until she was lying across his knees face down. She couldn't believe he meant it, she gave a gasping cry of shock as she felt his hand come down.

'I wasn't unfaithful to you,' he snapped, and hit her hard. 'There wasn't anyone else.' He hit her again and she writhed furiously, throwing herself backwards, so that she slid off his lap and tumbled to the floor, her red hair spilling over the carpet. Daniel was on top of her a second later and she hit him, with all the force she could muster, across his face. He took hold of her wrists, anchoring her to the floor by his knees, and she heaved upwards, panting breathlessly, trying to wrench free. One hand broke from his clasp, she flailed at him with it, flinging herself sideways again. Their bodies rolled over and over in confused, violent struggling. Lindsay punched and kicked and felt Daniel's hands trying to hold her, the heavy weight of his body forced down on her.

'Keep still, damn you,' he muttered, finally holding her down.

Through tousled masses of hair her eyes glared up at him, and unbelievably he started to laugh.

'You look like an old English sheepdog,' he said.

'I bite like one, too,' she threatened, showing him her teeth.

'I know, I've the toothmarks to prove it,' he said, and she reddened.

'That's a lie—I didn't bite you.'

He turned his head to one side, a finger touching his neck, and she saw the tiny mark in his skin and was taken aback, she couldn't remember doing it. 'What's that, then? A love bite?' he mocked, looking down at her, then his head swooped down and she caught her breath as she felt his mouth at her throat, his teeth gently nibbling her flesh. 'Tit for tat,' he whispered, then his lips pressed warmly, deeply, along the throbbing vein in her neck. 'You're crazy—there wasn't anyone else. Lindsay, believe me—there wasn't anyone. The last few months before you walked out, I was up to my ears in work. I didn't have time to eat or sleep, let alone go to bed with anyone else.'

'Or me?' Lindsay asked bitterly, and he held her face between his hands, staring into her eyes.

'You froze up on me, I didn't know why, did I? I was working flat out, all I knew was that suddenly I was getting cold looks from you, if I came near you, you went rigid and obviously didn't want to know.' He gave a rough sigh, his expression grim. 'We both leapt to conclusions. You decided I was sleeping around—I decided you'd either fallen out of love with me or were just plain frigid. Is that so surprising? Before we were married you jumped six feet in the air if I so much as tried to touch you.'

'I wanted you to,' she muttered, her face uncertain and flushed. 'I wasn't frigid, I was just nervous.'

'Inhibited,' Daniel said drily.

'Yes,' she said, because that was it in a nutshell. It had seemed so important then, the first time she would ever sleep with a man, it had looked like a unjumpable fence, she hadn't been able to make it. Angrily, she said: 'I wasn't very old, remember. It was the first time for me, and you scared me, you were so ...' Expert, she thought; he had been too experienced, it undermined her, she felt gauche and stupid when she thought of all the other women he had had, the sexy, exciting, sophisticated women from his own world who knew precisely what they were doing and made love with an expertise which matched his own. Lindsay had blushed and stammered and felt awkward and clumsy.

'I felt so boring,' she finished, and Daniel stared at her intently.

'You were lovely,' he whispered. 'Young and shy and adorable—I was almost afraid to touch you, I wanted you so much I was afraid of scaring you.'

'I was scaring myself,' she admitted. 'All the time—putting up barriers in my mind when what I really wanted to do was . . .'

'What?' he asked as she broke off, and she lifted her head and kissed him with a raw, open passion she had never shown him before. She felt the barriers in her head go down with a crash and the floodwaters poured over them, her arms went round him and her hands touched him the way she had been longing to touch him, her palms pressing into his body, her fingertips caressing and exploring along his spine, his nape, his shoulders. Daniel's hands slid under her and lifted her, held her so close they became one. Her robe fell open, he looked down at the smooth pale flesh and she heard his breathing quicken.

He stood up and the next second she was in his arms, carried close to him as he walked out of the room. He was looking at her every step of the way, he wasn't walking steadily, she felt him trembling and his deep chest heaved as if the air had no oxygen, he was snatching at every breath raggedly, while his eyes leapt over her naked body.

She felt as if it would be the first time, she was shaking as though in terror; but it was not fear, it was desire turning her limbs to water, tearing at her until she ached with longing.

Daniel put her down on the bed and began to pull off his clothes, his hands shaking. She watched, ice-cold suddenly with shock and piercing excitement, huddling in her robe to stop herself shivering. His body had a male power which her female instincts both recoiled from and were drawn towards, she couldn't stop looking at him, she was pale and at the same time feverish, her lips were dry, her breasts ached. She couldn't have spoken to save her life, and she didn't want him to speak, her whole being concentrated on a need to be part of him.

He knelt on the bed in the darkness, his eyes moving with nerve-racking slowness over her. His hand parted her robe, and she allowed it, her own hand falling back on the bed, palm curled upward, and Daniel stared as if he had never seen her, his pupils dilated, darkening his eyes and he breathed with parted lips, audibly. Lindsay couldn't move, she lay trembling, while he looked from the hollowed pallor of her shoulders to her warm, rounded breasts where the nipples had firmed, their pink surrounded by a darker circle, then down over her midriff and the flat, smooth stomach to her hips and slim thighs.

He was looking at her deliberately, it was an act of possession as much as would be the lovemaking which would follow, and Lindsay looked at him in hungry exploration in the same way.

When he put out his hand she tensed, watching. His fingers trailed softly where he chose to touch her, so light, so fleeting a contact, all the way down her body and a smothered gasp broke from her, she put up an arm to pull him down to her, the long-deferred desire too fierce to be borne. As he came down on her she shook violently and moaned in satisfaction, her arms round him, holding him locked to her.

Daniel lifted his head and caught her face in one hand, held it while he kissed her, but as if there was still anger somewhere in him it was not a gentle, tender kiss, it was a kiss of devouring intensity, bruising her mouth, forcing her head back against the pillow until her neck ached. She met it with fire, her lips clinging to his in burning response, and at last his mouth softened and warmed, he whispered: 'I love you, love you, you stupid little thing, there hasn't been anyone else, only you. I didn't want anyone else—I've tried to, but it didn't work, all I thought about was you.'

There was too much she wanted to say. I'm sorry, I've been stupid, I believe you, I love you, I'm such a fool.

She didn't say it, she said over and over again: 'I want you, I want you . . .'

'Oh,' Daniel muttered hoarsely as her body moved against him, her hands touching his shoulders, his chest, his strong thighs.

'I love you,' she said a second later on a wild

moan of pleasure as he entered her. 'Daniel, oh, Daniel!'

Words couldn't make the bridge on which they had to cross to become one being, their flesh melted and dissolved together, she felt the hair on the back of her neck prickling, her spine arching to meet the hardness of his body, and there were no inhibitions, no barriers left, because her fear had gone, taking them with it. She no longer feared other women, or her own inexperience and nervous shyness. Desire burnt them all out, both her own and his—she felt the agonising need in him as he took her, his breathing tortured by moans of intense pleasure. He had always been too strong, too sure of himself. Now he was neither; he was, like her, a human being drowning in sheer need, for the first time she felt they were on the same level, equal, moving together to the same goal.

No longer aware of what she was doing, she held him, her fingers digging into his back, her nails in his flesh, and Daniel groaned as though the pain delighted him, the urgent thrust of his body hurting and exciting her in turn.

She felt herself opening, the warm, receptive clamouring of her body engulfing him; the intensity rose to an unbearable peak, her deafened ears beat with her own cries, she did not hear the cries he gave, she moaned with closed eyes like someone dying and almost blacked out, her heart, brain, lungs seeming to cease their functions for an instant of time that seemed to stretch for ever.

Daniel's face was buried between her breasts

when she began to think again. He was hot, flushed, trembling violently. 'Darling, darling,' he kept saying, but his voice was low and hoarse, she only just heard him.

She put a trembling hand on his hair, it was damp with perspiration and clung to her fingers. 'I love you,' she said, stroking it, and he turned his head on her body, his lips brushing her skin.

'Do you believe . . .' he began, and she put a finger on his lips.

'I love you,' she said again, what else mattered? She had never understood the words before, she had mouthed them without knowing what she said, now she did, nobody in the world had ever said them or understood them as she did now. They were elastic, they contained whole dictionaries of meanings, when you loved you trusted, believed, accepted everything. She had wanted Daniel to prove himself, his love, she had greedily asked for all of him without giving all of herself; bargaining like a market stallholder, beating him down, when if she had really loved him she would have given to the end of the world without asking in return. She had set boundaries on her love and walled herself up inside them, now they had been smashed down and how she felt had washed over the whole world. She held the world in her arms when she held him. She was no *part* of him—she *was* him, and he was her, there were no divisions, no rights or claims between them, they were one being.

'I was crazy about you from the minute I saw you,' he said in a husky voice, kissing the finger muffling his words.

'I was too young,' she said. 'I didn't understand love. I do, now.'

'You do,' he agreed, and laughed. 'Oh yes, you do! I thought I was flying!'

There was that gentle mockery in his voice, and she smiled in the darkness, a hand running down his back and fingering the little indentations in his flesh where she had dug her nails into him without realising what she was doing. 'Daniel!' she exclaimed. 'Did I do these? I'm sorry, did I hurt you . . .'

'Mmm,' he said, kissing the little valley between her breasts. 'I loved it.'

'Wicked,' she said, laughing. 'That will teach you to blackmail people!'

He sighed, his body shifting so that he lay more easily against her, their bare legs entangled, his head still on her breasts but his weight not lying heavily on her. Lindsay felt him glancing up at her, his lashes flicking back.

'It seemed an irresistible opportunity,' he said wryly. 'I knew how much Stephen meant to you, you've always been very close, I figured you wouldn't be able to turn my offer down and I wanted you back at any price. When I saw you again, I knew I had to have you back, even if you hated me for it. You were lovely when you were five years younger, but now you're gorgeous.' His hand ran down her body from breast to thigh. 'Your figure was never this good before, you've rounded out beautifully. I couldn't take my eyes off you.'

'Or your hands,' Lindsay said in teasing dryness.

She felt him laughing. 'Or my hands,' he admitted without apparent shame. 'And when I kissed you I knew you were responding. I started to hope you still felt something, too. When I realised Stephen was in real trouble, I thought I'd use it to get you back. I wasn't sure exactly what was going on between you and Aston Hill.' He watched her sideways. 'I didn't think it meant much but I didn't like having him around. He was in love with you, wasn't he?'

'Poor Aston,' she said, frowning. 'Don't talk about him, it isn't fair to him.' She liked Aston far too much to discuss him with Daniel; Aston would hate that, it would be a betrayal of him, and Lindsay would hate to add insult to the injury she had done him.

'He didn't hide it,' Daniel told her. 'That night I bumped into him at the nightclub, he looked at me as if he'd like to kill me. I knew you must have told him something, I wasn't sure what, and I was afraid he might have hurt you, he seemed a very angry man and angry men get violent. That's why I rang—I'd have come round myself if I hadn't been with those Swedish guys.'

'Aston isn't the type to hit a woman,' Lindsay said, and Daniel grimaced.

'Not like me, you mean?'

'I shan't be able to sit down tomorrow,' she accused, but with a smile.

Daniel put a hand to his shoulder. 'I'm pretty black and blue, myself. You're a very violent lady.' He paused. 'If I hadn't turned up again, would you have married him?'

'Hypothetical questions are a waste of time,' Lindsay said.

'Would you?' Daniel pressed flatly, and she sighed.

'I don't know. I was never in love with him.'

He was quiet for a moment, then he said: 'I'm lucky I came back when I did. Another year and I reckon you'd have been married to him.'

'I didn't love him,' she insisted, and he nodded.

'Maybe not—you might have married him, all the same, and then all three of us would have been as miserable as sin.' He lifted his head, moving, and kissed her mouth possessively. 'Because you're mine and always have been, and sooner or later we would have met up again and once we saw each other we wouldn't have been able to stay apart. Hill may be as sick as death at the moment, but sooner or later he'll realise it was inevitable.'

'You were quite ruthless in the way you used Stephen against me, though,' Lindsay told him. 'That wasn't very nice, Daniel.'

'Lindsay, bailing Stephen out is a stupid undertaking, believe me—financially, I need my head examined. It will take years before his firm shows a profit—if it ever does. My accountants smile politely, but they look at me as if I'd gone mad. If they didn't know Stephen was your brother, they'd probably have me in a straitjacket by now. The accounts speak for themselves.'

'It was still completely immoral to blackmail me!'

'I'd have committed murder to get you back,'

he told her. 'A little blackmail seemed mild by comparison with what I wanted to do to Hill when I saw you kiss him at Stephen's house.' He looked at her, eyes glinting in the darkness. 'I love you,' he said, and she was silenced, the emotion in his voice held its own message, then he yawned and she began to laugh helplessly. 'Sorry,' he said. 'I'm used up, totally dead.' He yawned again widely and she pulled the covers over them, her arm cradling his head.

'Go to sleep then,' she said, feeling the warm, heavy weight of his body relaxing against her. This was how she had always wanted it; Daniel was hers, he belonged to her, and she belonged to him, but she had always been afraid of exposing herself by admitting the depth of her love because she could not have borne it if he left her once he knew. It would be different now. She was older, more sure of herself, more aware of what love meant. If there were problems ahead she would stand and face them, not run away, as she had before. If she had told him what was on her mind instead of walking away with her head in the air, they would never have parted. They hadn't known enough about each other, they hadn't talked enough, been honest enough. They had to learn so much, but they had already learnt the only vital thing—they loved each other.

Daniel was breathing in the regular rhythm of sleep, his naked body warm and slack in her arms, vulnerable, human, given up to her for safe keeping through the night. Lindsay let her own eyes close, a faint smile lingering along her mouth, and slowly drifted into sleep.

Harlequin Plus

A WORD ABOUT THE AUTHOR

Charlotte Lamb was born and raised in London's East End. To this day she remains at heart an unswerving Londoner, although for the past several years she has lived on the rain-swept Isle of Man in the Irish Sea. Charlotte likens the Isle of Man to the setting of Emily Brontë's *Wuthering Heights* and says that all one can see for miles around are "sheep and heather-covered moors."

Charlotte began writing romances in 1970. Her very first attempt was accepted by Mills & Boon, and she has never looked back.

Since those earlier days, she has become amazingly prolific. Always a fast typist, she can now create and commit to paper at least one novel a month! "I love to write, and it comes easily to me," she explains. "My books practically write themselves."

The fact that Charlotte has been married now for more than two decades, and is the devoted mother of five children ranging in age from seven to twenty, immediately brings to mind the question: where does she find the time to accomplish all her excellent writing? "I have a very good housekeeper," she says with a smile...as if that explains everything!

Harlequin Presents

ALL-TIME FAVORITE BESTSELLERS
...love stories that grow
more beautiful with time!

Now's your chance to discover the earlier great books in Harlequin Presents, the world's most popular romance-fiction series.

Choose from the following list.

Harlequin Presents

ALL-TIME FAVORITE BESTSELLERS

Complete and mail this coupon today!

Harlequin Reader Service

In the U.S.A.
P.O. Box 52040
Phoenix, Arizona 85072-9988

In Canada
649 Ontario Street
Stratford, Ontario N5A 6W2

Please send me the following Presents **ALL-TIME FAVORITE BESTSELLERS.** I am enclosing my check or money order for $1.75 for each copy ordered, plus 75¢ to cover postage and handling.

☐ #17	☐ #38	☐ #50	☐ #67	☐ #75
☐ #20	☐ #41	☐ #54	☐ #70	☐ #78
☐ #32	☐ #42	☐ #62	☐ #71	☐ #83
☐ #35	☐ #46	☐ #66	☐ #73	

Number of copies checked @ $1.75 each = $ _____
N.Y. and Ariz. residents add appropriate sales tax $ _____
Postage and handling $ __.75__
TOTAL $ _____

I enclose _____
(Please send check or money order. We cannot be responsible for cash sent through the mail.)
Prices subject to change without notice.

NAME _____
(Please Print)

ADDRESS _____ APT. NO. _____

CITY _____

STATE/PROV. _____

ZIP/POSTAL CODE _____

Offer expires April 30, 1984   31056000000